# Wrong Time, Wrong Place

by

## Jeff Resnick

PublishAmerica
Baltimore

First printing

At the specific preference of the author, PublishAmerica allowed this work to remain exactly as the author intended, verbatim, without editorial input.

ISBN: 1-4137-8514-X
PUBLISHED BY PUBLISHAMERICA, LLLP
www.publishamerica.com
Baltimore

Printed in the United States of America

# Other Books by Jeff Resnick

Non-Fiction:

*Secrets: Unlocking the Mysteries of Successful Advertising*
*www.jeffresnick.com/advert/secrets_mediareps.html*

Fiction:

*Stardust*
*www.jeffresnick.com/advert/stardust.html*

## Jeff's CD's

*Standards, Vol. 1-5*
*www.jeffresnick.com/music/cd.html*

*For Emma, Caden, and Chelsea*

To Bil Boom,
   Good luck in your
sound sculpture!

   Time stands still...
we merely move through it.

To Bil Brown,
Good luck in your
second sculpture!

...Time stands still...
as surely race through it

# Prologue

Well, well, well! It seems quite some time ago that I told you Woody Reed would describe his first journey to The Zone, in his own words. Give this young man an inch and he takes a mile! Of course, he was always like that, even as a youngster practicing his saxophone hour upon hour. Tell him it's time to quit and you could see that momentary flicker of rebellion in his eyes. I'll never forget that first wedding gig when Trumpet Man called out "The Party's Over" as the last song of the evening. Woody was only twelve years old at the time, not yet wise to the inner workings of his creative mind, not to mention all the creative energies surrounding him. Woody's young eyes told the story, all right. You just knew he didn't want to stop, undoubtedly *couldn't* stop the creative flow in midstream at the drop of a hat. And why *should* he, when you get right down to it? Life demands that we rebel against what we seem so unable to comprehend. Is it wrong to try so desperately to hang on to those rare moments of revelation?

Didn't you ever wonder why Jazz musicians, *real* musicians, if you will, have such a hard time *coming down* after a gig? It's all about reveling in the moment. Just think about what it takes to achieve that moment in the first place. No wonder it's so hard to let go of it. Yes, I guess I'm not surprised that Woody would go on and on as he did, unable to turn the faucet off once opened. You see I've been where he now is. I've experienced the same revelations and understandings. I know of what I speak. In fact, I could tell you firsthand what it's like on *both* sides of the inner doors, the one side Woody has already visited on several occasions, and the other side where I now *reside,* for want of a better word. And at some time yet to come, perhaps I will feel obliged to tell you about where and how I exist within the framework of our misunderstood world. But this moment is not that time. There is simply too much for you to learn before you'll be ready to accept the truth of it all.

If you think back, you'll recall that Woody and Violetta were performing at The Ellicott Club. Violetta took a few moments seating herself at stage front, all the while mouthing words to herself that no one else could possibly hear or hope to understand. Her audience hushed as she placed her cane on the floor behind her stool, then made sure her guitar was perfectly in tune. At that moment, the house lights were lowered to candle light, the stage lights were raised to full brightness, and Violetta began her performance without a word of introduction. By about the second or third song, Woody sensed that she was, as he described it at the time, distracted. Not to the point where anyone in the audience would ever notice, but he couldn't help but wonder why she seemed only on the edge of focus, as if something more important was on her mind. It showed itself in little ways, like her eyes darting in the surprised moment of a forgotten lyric, or her fingers refusing to move in complete synch with her musical thoughts. She seemed to be fighting with herself to maintain her composure, her marvelous musicianship barely managing to win out in the end at the expense of her stamina.

Violetta's dilemma couldn't help but add a frightening sense of fragility to Woody's own already frayed nerves. There could have been nothing worse than to have to stand alone in the dark, waiting backstage to join Violetta for the second half of the performance, wanting nothing more than to rescue her from whatever was closing in on her so oppressively. Through it all, she kept glancing over to where Woody was standing, though she surely couldn't see him, given the contrast of the bright spotlights on stage to the suffocating darkness offstage. For what it was worth, Woody concentrated on her music as strongly as he could, hoping his own thoughts would somehow help her conquer whatever unseen demons were torturing her soul and undoubtedly testing her resolve.

Those first thirty minutes seemed like thirty hours, and by the time Violetta turned her head towards Woody one last time to make sure he hadn't run away, he felt emotionally drained, physically spent, but surely only a fraction of what she must have been feeling. Perhaps that explains why at that moment in time, something inside of Woody seemed to kick in, demanding his creative inner self to be at its strongest for Violetta's sake. This would be *his* time in the spotlight, not to steal it from her, but to rescue her from it. Where she was weak, he would be strong. Where she had doubts, he would be confident. Where she stumbled, he would fly. Where she was fearful, he would be bold. Woody stepped forward far enough to the edge of the stage that Violetta alone could see him, and he clenched his fists in front of his face in a gesture of strength, willing her to take power from his unspent reserves. When she saw him, even at that distance he could see her eyes welling up with tears, and her expression seemed to say '*thank God you didn't run away, Woody...I need you.*' Woody slowly mouthed the three words whose strength he knew she needed to feel, carefully accenting each syllable.

9

'*I…Love…You*'.

Woody saw the dark clouds of uncertainty evaporating from Violetta's place beneath the bright lights. She exhaled loudly, and her demeanor took on the same resolute look that Woody remembered from their conversation about the trauma of losing her parents in that irrevocable drunken instant. As then, she smiled, once again as if indicating that the hard part was over, and it was time to regain control of her emotions. With that, she took the microphone in hand and began to speak to her audience, not merely as a musical artist addressing paying customers, but as a human confiding her inner-most feelings and insecurities to her closest friends.

"I can't tell you how wonderful it is to come back to The Ellicott Club again," she began, "to be around all of my dearest friends. I'm sure you know I love you as much as you love me, maybe more!"

The audience responded with knowing smiles and gentle applause, letting her know they felt the same way. And when Violetta again spoke, they remained totally silent, with not a word of distracting conversation to be heard.

"I must be honest with you…the past few days have been very strange…and at the same time, very beautiful. If I seem a bit off the musical mark this evening, it's because I have learned things about life that I never could have imagined. You see, I now know, we are not alone in this world."

The only sound Woody could hear was the soft electric buzz of the spotlights, accentuated by breaths being held in anticipation amid the absence of any physical motion. Even the tuxedoed waiters remained frozen in place at the back of the room by her words. She lowered her gaze to the floor for only a brief instant, then graced her audience with a most lovely smile as she began to lightly strum her guitar with sustained chords as she again spoke. Woody recognized the strummed backdrop as "My One and Only Love."

"Before I get *completely* maudlin," she continued, strumming as she spoke, "I have a *very* special surprise planned for you tonight. Most of you knew my parents from their time performing here on this very stage where I'm now sitting. And you know that I miss them terribly, as you do. Some of you also know me well enough to understand that after they left us, I put an emotional wall up around myself, not allowing anyone else *in* to share my troubles...*or* my joys. Until now, that is," she said in a whisper, again turning her head to look at Woody offstage, many in the audience craning to follow her gaze but unable to locate the object of her attention in the darkness offstage.

"It is my sincere pleasure to introduce you to a wonderful musician," she said, "a loving and caring man who has captured my heart in a way I never thought would be possible. I ask you, now, to please welcome Mr. Woody Reed...my one and only love...as he joins me on stage in front of this roomful of my dearest friends."

All eyes were fixed on Woody as he dragged his trembling body across what seemed a six-mile long stage to join Violetta, who had by then concluded her six-string introduction. When he finally reached stage front, the hall seemed deathly quiet, the reverberation of his footsteps on the wooden floor the uncanny center of attention. Woody got down on one knee beside her, held her left hand in both of his, leaned forward and kissed her ever so gently and gentlemanly on the lips. After what seemed much too long a moment, he stood back up to see she was staring at him, her moist emerald eyes lustrous in the spotlight. They both turned to face their audience, together, ready to begin their first professional performance as a duo, startled to see women and men alike reaching for handkerchiefs to wipe away their own tears as they surely remembered Violetta's *other* first professional performance on this stage, that with her parents. All at once, the palpable barrier that had until this moment stifled any sound or movement suddenly fell away, for the hall erupted into thunderous applause, having nothing to do with music, since they hadn't as yet played a note together! Woody grasped Violetta's hand once more as the two of them graciously accepted the audience's show of unconditional love. Glancing over at Violetta on her stool at his side, Woody was relieved to see that this show of affection was just what she needed to reinvigorate her soul. Borrowing a page from The Performer's book of tricks, on a whim he took the microphone, hoping to move them forward into the actual show. The very fact that he was ready to joke with the audience clearly indicated a dramatic change in his own life, for he had never before understood the value of showmanship.

"Ladies and gentlemen," he began. "Thank you so much for your generous applause."

Woody waited a full 30 seconds for the hand clapping to die down before continuing.

"Violetta and I thoroughly enjoyed performing for you this evening. We had a wonderful time. Thank you again…and good night!"

Woody abruptly turned to exit the stage, feigning an attempt to pull Violetta with him by her hand. By now, she was laughing hysterically, pulling back doubly hard on his hand with both of hers to prevent him from leaving the stage. Not surprisingly, the audience reacted as expected, uproariously, genuinely appreciating this meager attempt at a little vaudevillian humor to lighten the mood. Thankfully, it also served to let them know that it was time to proceed with the show, and the laughter turned to chuckles, finally relenting to sighs as everyone settled back into their seats to enjoy the music yet to come. Violetta immediately started playing the introduction to their first song together without bothering to tell Woody what it was.

All it took were the first three words she sang for him to know she had selected a Cole Porter classic, "I Love You," as if to repeat the same words Woody had mouthed to her from offstage only a few minutes ago. This young woman certainly knew how to tug the heartstrings.

For the next hour, Violetta and Woody journeyed from composer to composer, and decade to decade. Now fully revitalized, Violetta stared at Woody for a brief moment after every song, causing him some concern, since he had no idea what might motivate her to do that. She seemed to be gauging his reactions, wondering to herself if what she had in mind for them was indeed about to happen, perhaps unsure if she dare venture there without him. As the time approached 9:30, they as yet hadn't performed "Stardust," and Woody sensed that she was not only saving it for last, but also purposely withholding it from him as a lover holds back the ultimate moment of ecstasy as long as possible. Alas, the time had arrived and she would wait no longer, easing into the introduction flawlessly.

As she sang, she was staring directly at Woody, and he held her eyes with his own while he wove his musical answers around her voice ever so softly, oblivious to the presence of anyone else in the room except the two of them. They knew where this musical foreplay was destined to lead. All their thoughts were focused on the moment, and for them, any sense of time and place ceased to exist.

'I love you, Violetta,' Woody thought in his mind.

'And I love you, Woody,' she answered without words.

13

Their eyes never left each other as they began their much anticipated ascent, all the while maintaining their physical performance on stage. And then the strangest and yet most beautiful thing happened. At precisely the same instant, they both looked to the audience as they rose to see all eyes fixed on their stage presence, oblivious to the ascending auras that no one could possibly see or experience, locked out of Woody and Violetta's dimension as the audience was. All except one pair of eyes, that is. How wonderful, how amazing, how uplifting it was to see Lenny Dee's eyes following them upward, arthritic fingers steepled to his mouth as if in prayer, knowing in his heart exactly where they were headed, thankful that he had lived to see the fulfillment of his promise to Violetta's father.

Woody heard Violetta's voice in his mind.

'Woody, Trumpet Man told me about the inner doors. Since meeting him, I've prayed they would be revealed to me.'

In that very moment, Woody truly understood The Gift he had been given, and he foresaw the beautiful secret mission that he was about to fulfill. Violetta held fast to him, not letting him escape from her mind, which, of course, he had no intention of doing anyway. The inner doorway appeared before them in their common thoughts. For the briefest instant, Woody sensed her hesitation, as if fearful of what awaited them, but this passed in the flicker of an eyelid. Without need of physical movement, they *willed* themselves through, together, knowing they had successfully entered when the doorway disappeared from their thoughts. Violetta's emotions were Woody's emotions, their spirits one and the same, inseparable, as his mind heard the two voices…whispering…in unison…

'Violetta'…

…followed so tenderly by his love's answer…

'Mama…Papa…'

Together, they had successfully entered The Zone, that magical place to which all improvisatory musicians seek to travel every time they set foot on stage, where they experienced that emotional and long-awaited reunion with Violetta's deceased parents. I should probably also tell you that Violetta and Woody didn't remain very long on the other side of the inner door that was opened to them, at least not on this visit. After all, they had another show to perform in but 22 hours! Once they had completed their journey and descended to The Ellicott Club's stage, they rejoined that moment in your time at the conclusion of "Stardust." They made a hasty retreat, apologizing to their host and guests alike that they were too exhausted from the performance to remain for cocktails, food, or conversation. As they prepared to leave for their necessary recuperative and restorative sleep at Woody's apartment, Lenny Dee gently pulled Woody aside. He stuffed something into Woody's shirt pocket, and with a tear in his eye, he waved a bent index finger in Woody's direction as he issued a grave warning.

"Don' you *ever* tell my Violetta I dun dis, or you gonna be in *big* trouble, you unnerstan' me?"

Woody stood there, flabbergasted, unsure how to respond, whereupon Lenny abruptly turned and hurried away, nearly tripping over his too-long pant legs, before losing control of his emotions entirely. Woody reached into his pocket to find two crisp hundred-dollar bills wrapped around a hand-written note, signed by Lenny.

Violetta was right.
I ain't never heard anyone play so good as you.
Her Mama & Papa must love you...
See you tomorrow night, kid.
Lenny Dee

15

Without a second thought, Woody absent-mindedly stuffed the bills and note into his pants pocket before leaving the Ellicott Club that evening with Violetta.

The first thing Woody did the next day was to call Cassie, the wife of his deceased mentor, Trumpet Man. Cassie was eager to hear of Woody's escapades since she had last seen him, scolding him that it was much too long ago. He could hear little Emma Jane in the background excitedly asking whom her Nana was talking to on the phone. Hearing her giggle, Woody could only conjure up images of another Emma Jane he had just met, this one in Williamsburg. How strange would it be to see Trumpet Man's granddaughter after so much time had passed? How much like the *other* Emma Jane would she be? To Violetta's embarrassment, all Woody could talk about on the phone was meeting her. Cassie invited both of them to visit on Sunday, promising that her daughters and their families would be invited as well. She was not about to let Woody escape town without giving her the chance to meet this woman he obviously loved so deeply.

In truth, Woody would spend many hours agonizing over how much to reveal to this woman whom he had avoided for so many years, for reasons you now understand. Should he tell her about his travels to The Zone? More importantly, would he tell her about his otherworldly contacts in the vestibule and beyond with his deceased mentor, her beloved husband, Trumpet Man? You'll recall that even the Williamsburg clan had not even the slightest inkling of The Performer's travels to those same places.

This is where I now pick up on the thread of this remarkable story. I must warn you, however, that all is not as it seemed. It never is. For strange things are about to happen...but I get ahead of myself by attempting to simplify things so early in the telling! Suffice it to say you will experience some disorientation as this tale unfolds, much the same as Woody experiences. In time, the contradictions you encounter will be explained to you. But you have no choice other than to find the answers to the mysteries presented along with Woody, for his journey is also one of confusion and revelation. You will come to realize the answers as he does. After all, Woody is living the story in real time with no means of narrating to you what he himself can not yet know. So be patient. The truth will ultimately be revealed to you.

As before, I will let Woody tell you in his own words what he is experiencing as he is living it. His story is indeed a fascinating one. Your presence here is testament to that, is it not?

# Chapter One

*Woody*

I awoke Saturday afternoon, well rested after an uninterrupted fourteen hours of restorative sleep. By now a veteran traveler to The Zone, I no longer required as much time to recuperate as Violetta, she a relative novice to this form of travel. We were wise not to tarry long in that place, knowing that we were scheduled to perform at the Ellicott Club once again on Saturday evening, that being but a few short hours from now.

I opened my eyes to get my bearings. My left arm was still draped around Violetta's shoulder, her back to me. I lay there unmoving for several minutes, savoring the warmth of her body, the sweet smell of her auburn hair on my face, and the slow pace of her breathing. I had no doubt that Violetta would want to talk at length about our experience last night beyond the inner door that was revealed to us. I also had no doubt that she would hold off on broaching the subject of being reunited there at long last with her parents for as long as she could, not wanting to break the magical spell she surely felt surrounding her. I gently untangled myself, careful not to wake her, and quietly padded off to the kitchen of my small apartment, where we had decided to spend the weekend. I brewed a fresh pot of cinnamon hazelnut coffee, my favorite. The delightful aroma must have accomplished what I didn't have the heart to do, for Violetta soon joined me at the small kitchen table, wearing my green flannel robe to keep her warm. She smiled at me, unable to hide the wonderment she must have felt deep down in her soul.

"Good morning, Woody," she whispered with a twinkle of emerald green eyes.

"It certainly is," I answered softly.

She ambled over to my chair and sat on my lap without need of invitation, nuzzling her head on my shoulder warmly. We sat there in complete silence for several minutes, feeling no need to do anything but snuggle and smell the coffee brewing.

"Thank you, Woody," she whispered in my ear.

"For what?" I asked innocently, pulling my head back so I could see her eyes.

"For last night," she continued. "I knew what was about to happen. And I knew that *you* knew why I had saved 'Stardust' for our last song of the evening. But communicating with my parents was...well...the most wonderful and beautiful thing that has ever happened to me. Aside from meeting you, that is," she half-joked lightly.

"It was quite a ride, wasn't it?" I laughed.

"It certainly was, Woody."

"Are you hungry, Violetta?"

"I could eat a horse!"

"I thought so," I said, knowing exactly how she felt after an exhausting journey to The Zone. "What do you say we have a cup of coffee here, then go out for a late lunch before heading over to the club?"

"Sounds good to me," she offered, getting up to pour us each a cup of coffee.

After only a few forced gulps, Violetta shuffled off to the bathroom to shower, leaving me to enjoy the flavored coffee that she obviously didn't care for. I, on the other hand, reveled in each swallow. Once I heard the shower running in the bathroom, I decided to call Trumpet Man's wife, Cassie, to re-establish contact after so many years. After all, the last time I saw her was when I had performed "Stardust" at Trumpet Man's funeral so many years ago. Yet it seemed like only yesterday.

Cassie picked up on the fourth ring. I couldn't help but recognize her voice.

"Hullo?" she answered.

"Cassie?" I asked.

"Yes...who is this?" she wondered aloud.

"Cassie...it's Woody," I managed to say not at all convincingly, somehow unable to get any more than three words out. There was silence on the other end, as if she was wrestling with what she had just heard. Afraid she might hang up, I blurted out, "Cassie, it's Woody Reed...I know it's been a long time, but...I would *really* like to come over and see you and Emma Jane before I go back out on the road."

"Lordy, lordy," Cassie bellowed. "I should hang up on you right now, young man, for not calling in so many years! What have you been up to?"

"Cassie, I wouldn't know where to begin...but I want you to meet someone very special," I stammered.

"Would this very special person be a young lady?" she asked, purposely drawing out each word as her voice rose in pitch.

"Yes, she would be. I know you'll love her, Cassie...because I do. She's the best thing that's ever happened to me..."

As I gushed on about Violetta, I felt her presence behind me without even hearing her enter the room. I turned around quickly in mid-sentence and saw her standing there, wrapped in a towel, straining to hear what I was saying. I felt my face heat up and turn beet red, and gave Violetta a resigned look of embarrassment, shrugging my shoulders for want of anything else to do. Violetta had obviously heard enough of my conversation to share the feeling, for her cheeks were equally colored by now. I turned back around to concentrate on Cassie's answer, whereby she invited me to bring Violetta over to visit tomorrow afternoon to meet her.

"I have so much I want to tell you, Cassie," I said, leaning towards revealing my encounters with Trumpet Man in the vestibule of The Zone during the past week, but not wanting to share such a powerful moment over the telephone.

"Oh, and I have so much to tell *you*, Woody!" she laughed loudly.

"*Realllly*," I joked. "What's up?"

"Ohhh, you'll see, Woody," she concluded. "I've got someone for *you* to meet, too…actually, *two* someones!"

I couldn't imagine whom she might be talking about, realizing I'd need to wait until the next day to satisfy my curiosity.

"Okay, then, we'll see you tomorrow around three, Cassie," I chuckled, breaking the connection before turning back to Violetta, only to realize that she had silently retreated to the bedroom. Within minutes she was back in the kitchen, squeaky clean, fully dressed and ready to go. I took that as my cue to follow her lead and showered as quickly as she had, toweling off with little regard for the droplets of water left untouched when I threw my jeans and sweatshirt on. While I was in the bathroom, Violetta cleaned up the kitchen, leaving it immaculate in a way that I never could have…or, would have.

We threw our coats on, locked the door, and walked down the front stairs, bracing ourselves for the cold winter wind that would surely sting our faces as we hopped in my car before she thought to utter a word.

"Where we goin'?" she asked, more to break the uncomfortable silence of wanting to ask me who I had been talking to on the phone than wanting to know our destination.

"I know this little place down on Park Avenue called the Toad Lagoon," I told her as I started the car.

"The Toad Lagoon? That's a strange name for a restaurant," she laughed.

"Actually, the real name of the place is the Frog Pond, but for some reason I could never seem to remember that, so I always called it the Toad Lagoon. Close enough for Jazz, right? Anyway, they have the best oat pancakes you've ever tasted, Violetta! They make 'em with a special butter milk batter and load 'em up with nuts and raisins with a shake of confectioner's sugar on top. Add a little butter and a lot of maple syrup, and you'll feel full for a week," I promised.

Arriving at the Toad Lagoon at about 3 o'clock was a good thing. Had we showed up during lunch or dinner, we would have had to wait at least an hour for a table. But our timing was perfect, for we had our choice of empty booths. We threw our coats over the metal coat rack next to the door and sat down without need of looking at the menu, for I had already decided what we would order.

"Hi Woody," the waitress said with a smile and a wink as she approached our table. "I haven't seen you in a while…been on the road?"

"Hey, Briggett," I answered in return, realizing once again that I was blushing mightily, though I certainly had no reason to. "Yeah, as a matter of fact, I have."

Not wanting Violetta to feel left out I took her hand in mine and made the required introductions.

"Briggett, I'd like you to meet Violetta. Violetta, meet Briggett."

They exchanged polite smiles before Briggett left with our double order of oat pancakes, heavy on the maple syrup, light on the butter.

"Briggett?" Violetta asked coyly, one eyebrow raised as if expecting a tell-all true confession.

"Puleeze," I blushed. "Briggett and I have been friends ever since I started coming here for breakfast years ago," I said as innocently as possible. "Honest," I pleaded in a final attempt to put her tease to rest.

With that, Violetta and I spent the next hour devouring our oat pancakes and enjoying the kind of coffee that puts hair on your chest. Every now and then, I caught a glimpse of Briggett out of the corner of my eye, watching our every move, smiling at me whenever she thought I would notice her attention. I can't be sure if Violetta noticed. But knowing women as I now do, I wouldn't be surprised if she had logged every glance in her mental notebook.

# Chapter Two

The longer we sat and talked after oat pancakes and coffee, the more uncomfortable I became. The hour was growing late, and I knew there could be nothing worse than arriving late for any gig, let alone this one, finding oneself in the position of not having adequate time to mentally prepare for the kind of performance we both wanted to deliver. All at once, Violetta took my hand in hers from across the table, drawing the conversation on for far too long.

"Woody," she began hesitantly. "Do you think...I mean, would you mind if I saved 'Stardust' to close out our show again tonight?"

I knew this moment would come sooner or later. Sensing her angst, I stared directly into her eyes as I answered as patiently as possible, careful not to add to the stress she was putting upon herself.

"Violetta, I don't mind at all. I know what a wonderful experience it was for you. And for me as well. I just don't want you to be disappointed if it doesn't happen again, so easily, and so soon after last night," I cautioned, attempting to prevent her from setting herself up for the kind of failure that could surely devastate her soul.

Her eyes lowered from my stare as she spoke. As they did, I realized that she was actually stalling, not wanting, or perhaps afraid, to leave. This began to cause me more than a little nervousness, for we were already cutting it pretty tight before our 7:30 show time. Torn between my own task-oriented inner clock and my efforts not to cause her any more discomfort, I relented to the conversation at hand, hoping we could still make it to the Ellicott Club with time to spare.

"I know, Woody. You're right," she continued. "It's all I can do not to pray that we journey there tonight. I just want so desperately to communicate with my parents again. All these years, I knew they were looking for me but just didn't how to contact me. Since meeting you, and performing with you, it's like a dream come true, Woody," Violetta confided softly.

"Truly, a dream," I agreed, realizing that I had to grab the bull by the horns and get us out of here at once, lest we miss our show entirely. With that thought uppermost in my mind, I gently removed my hand from her grasp, slid out of the booth and stood, indicating it was time to leave. As if on cue, Briggett approached and handed me the check along with her parting words.

"I hope I see you again soon, Woody," she smiled mischievously.

"Oh, you'll see *both* of us real soon, Briggett," I answered without hesitation, realizing I needed to nip this little game in the bud.

"It was nice meeting you, Violetta," Briggett said without much conviction, but at least politely.

"You too, Briggett," Violetta responded as she got up from the booth, cane in hand.

I didn't dare look back as we walked out the door, certain I would see Briggett watching us from inside. I threw my arm

25

around Violetta's shoulder to keep her warm in the cold air. She leaned into me easily, and we shuffled our way to the car. Heavy, wet snowflakes were beginning to descend, visible in the streetlights, showering the sidewalk with the warm glow of a winter evening. Violetta sighed loudly, smiling at the same time.

"Just friends, huh?" she joked as she flung her arm around my waist.

"Yup. Just friends," I repeated.

I opened the car door for her and she smiled. I winked down at her, closed her door, and walked around to the driver's side. To my surprise, the door was locked when I attempted to open it. I knew I hadn't locked it. I peeked through the closed window to see Violetta smiling teasingly before she finally reached over and unlocked the door she had just locked while I was walking around the car.

"Ohhh, Violetta," I swooned mockingly. "I can see this is gonna be a funny evening."

We both enjoyed a good chuckle as I started the car and pulled away from the curb. We didn't speak at all on the way back to my apartment, where we needed to gather our clothes and instruments before driving to the club. Once on the way again, we remained silent still, not from disinterest, but from the pull we both were beginning to feel in our hearts. It was time to put our performance face on, much like an athlete puts on his game face.

By the time we arrived at The Ellicott Club it was already 7 p.m. Lenny Dee was pacing like a caged animal, waiting to pounce on us as we entered the lobby. Managing to control his temper, he jerked his thumb towards the dressing room without saying a word. Knowing we had cut it much too close for our 7:30 show time, we hurried to the dressing room to change into the clothes that were in the garment bag slung over my shoulder. Between our clothes, her guitar case, and my saxophone case, I was pretty winded as she opened the dressing room door. I couldn't shake the strange feeling in my gut. This was too rushed. With everything that had happened to us, so quickly, not to mention Violetta's anticipation of journeying to The Zone once again, the world just felt a little out of sync. Glancing at Violetta as she applied her stage make-up, I could sense the nervousness in her face. I was about to leave the dressing room to give her some needed space and time alone before our performance when there was a knock on the door. Before I could even reach for the doorknob, Lenny Dee came barreling in, only adding to the strangeness of the evening.

"Lissen, youse two," he squealed in that high pitched voice. "I was tinkin' it might be better for da two of youse to do da whole show toget'er tonight. No need to keep 'em waitin' for da kid to come on stage later, Violetta. Everyone sure loved you bot' last night, y'know?"

Disturbed from her pre-concert routine, Violetta was obviously shaken by Lenny's intrusive entrance so close to show time. She just nodded blankly before returning her attention to the image in the mirror in front of her. I knew this evening was going downhill fast. After Lenny left the dressing room, I walked over to Violetta, kissed her on the forehead, and did my best to calm her down.

"You'll be fine, Violetta," I consoled.

"Woody...if anything happens tonight, you won't...I mean...please don't leave me alone," she pleaded.

"Not a chance, my love," I answered. "And nothing is going to happen. Just concentrate on doing a great show. Everything else will follow in its own way."

I realized that my own words didn't sound all that convincing even to myself, and I suspect Violetta took little comfort from them. There was another knock on the door.

"Five minutes, Violetta," announced the stage manager without entering the dressing room.

She looked at me, unable to hide the panic she must have been feeling about what was about to take place...or not.

# Chapter Three

"Show time," echoed the disembodied voice from the hallway outside the dressing room, followed by a single loud and intrusive knock.

I bent forward and lifted my sax from its velvet-lined case, suspecting I would soon be in the position of physically needing all the warmth it could offer. Violetta was still staring into the mirror, oblivious to anything going on around her.

"Violetta," I whispered so as not to startle her. "You look absolutely beautiful tonight, even more than usual," I lied, hoping to lift her spirits but failing miserably.

She turned towards me and gave me a look that seemed to ask *'did you just say something?'* Not knowing what else to do, I opened the dressing room door, waving my right arm across the threshold in a gesture that was meant to indicate it was time to leave the confines of this room. It took several moments for her to realize where she was and what I was doing, standing there like a marble statue with one arm in front of the open doorway and the other holding my saxophone. After a flicker of recognition, she stood and limped past me, out the door, into the hallway.

"Uhhh…Violetta…did you forget something?" I asked in as close to a joking tone of voice as I could muster, immediately recognizing that any attempt at humor was misplaced under these circumstances.

She just looked at me as if in a daze, with not a clue of what I had just asked her. So, I planted my foot against the door to prop it open and reached back to grab her guitar from its stand, somehow managing not to drop my old big-bell Conn in the process. She wordlessly took the guitar from me before abruptly turning away and setting off towards the stage in stiff, robot-like movements. I followed close behind, not knowing if I should say anything more.

The closer we got to the back stage area, the more we could hear the intensity of voices coming from those already seated in the audience, awaiting the show they had all surely heard about from those in attendance last night. It's funny, but you can get a real feel for your audience before you even set foot on stage. Last night's pre-concert buzz was subdued and affectionate. This evening's sounds were almost raucous, ripe with expectation, challenging us performers to deliver on the unspoken promise of an excellent show. I could hear the Master of Ceremonies concluding his introduction of us on stage.

"Ladies and gentlemen," he bellowed, "without further adieu, please welcome the Ellicott Club's own beloved artist of the guitar and voice…Violetta…accompanied this evening by brilliant tenor saxophonist Woody Reed!"

How strange that I actually laughed out loud at his choice of words. I was not yet ready to consider myself *brilliant* by any stretch of the imagination. In that final moment before our feet would transport us onto the stage without even thinking about the required steps, I placed my arm around Violetta's shoulder in a final gesture of physical support and emotional encouragement. I was startled by the instant realization that she was shaking, her skin cold to my touch.

"I'm right beside you, my love," I whispered in her ear without removing my arm from her shoulder.

She stepped forward without looking at me, as if steeling her resolve. And then it happened. Her leg, so badly mangled years ago in the car accident that had claimed her parents' lives, caught on the threshold at the rear of the stage. My world seemed to grind down into a vision of agonizing slow motion. I saw her start to fall forward, trying desperately to cradle her guitar. I heard the audience gasp in horror, such an abrupt shift from their loud applause only a moment ago in time. Before I was aware of a conscious thought to do anything, I lunged forward, roughly inserting my hand under her right arm to prevent her fall. While she had been rescued, the guitar was not so lucky, eluding her last second protective grab and slipping to the floor with a loud klunk, causing yet another gasp from the guests. I quickly bent over and picked it up, inspecting it for any damage before I handed it back to Violetta.

To my surprise, her guitar survived its fall with not even a scratch in sight. However, Violetta's psyche was another story. She just stood there, staring *through* her guitar, unsure what to do next. I placed my arm around her waist from behind, steadying her, and guided her to the seat awaiting her at stage front. I was totally conscious of the murmurs coming from the audience. People were still standing, craning their necks to get a better look at what was going on in front of their incredulous eyes.

The lighting technician must have been equally confused and unsure of protocol, for he dimmed the stage lights in his confusion and brought the house lights back up to full. Once I had Violetta seated, I got down on one knee, blocking view of her from the audience as much as possible, and looked her directly in the eyes.

"Violetta...my love...I'm here for you," I whispered as reassuringly as possible. "I will be your strength. Lean on me, for I'll never let you down."

A tentative smile, intended for me only but seen by many others as well, ventured through the tears she couldn't hold back. Seeing that, the audience began a slow rhythmic applause which built in intensity when the lighting tech realized this must be his unseen cue to dim the house lights and raise the stage lights back to full brilliance. This show would go on after all. As I stood back up and turned to face the audience, I was struck as if by a slap in the face that Violetta hadn't executed her usual habit of silently mouthing words of comfort to herself, unheard by all except her intended parental recipients in another world. This, after all, had become her tradition before performing, and her failure to remain true to procedure, no matter how strange it might seem to anyone else, was not a good omen.

I knew that Violetta would need at least a few moments to gather her wits. I decided to repeat last evening's tactic of addressing the crowd with my humble attempt at a bit of vaudevillian humor. My sax securely attached to its neck strap and hanging safely in front of me, I took the microphone in my right hand, placing my left hand in my pocket in a typical gesture of casual confidence. To my surprise, I felt a wad of paper crinkling from my touch, realizing I had forgotten to remove Lenny Dee's note and cash after last night's show. I think I even smiled at the absurdity of the moment.

"Ladies and gentlemen," I began. "Thank you so much for coming to hear Violetta and me perform this evening. I hope you've had as much fun as we have, for we thoroughly enjoyed playing for you. Thank you again, and please drive home safely."

I turned back to Violetta, tugging on her arm in a comic gesture of attempting to drag her off stage against her will. Last night the audience had responded with uproarious laughter and applause. They *got it.* Tonight's audience responded with dead silence.

*'If only The Performer could see me now,'* I thought while standing there as if naked, heartbeat pounding in my ears, my lips responding with an uncomfortable self-protective attempt at a smile.

Violetta apparently had decided to rescue me this time, for she began strumming her guitar lightly behind me. My first thought was to get down on my hands and knees and thank her for saving me from the abject embarrassment I had brought upon myself. My second thought was the realization that she was leading us into "Stardust" as the first song of the evening. I felt an overwhelming dread, spiraling down into a bottomless vortex, totally out of control, out of sync, and at the mercy of forces beyond my comprehension.

When Violetta began singing the introspective introduction to "Stardust," her voice quivered nervously, searching in vain for the meaning in the words she was mouthing from habit, not emotion. It was wrong. Everything about tonight was wrong. Playing this song now was wrong, for it was Violetta's undisguised attempt at escape from the moment, casting away any hope of an emotional performance in search of a journey that was not to be offered for the wrong reasons. I closed my eyes, knowing that any rescue this night would have to come from me. Violetta was just not up to it.

In the middle of her tortured introduction, I jumped in assertively with an *'I'll take it from here'* attitude, letting her know she need not sing again until ready. She settled into a thankful if not pleasant accompaniment behind me, realizing that on this evening I would be the one bearing the burden of performance. Little by little, I found a comfortable musical groove despite the shaky start to the evening. As the notes began to cascade from my old Conn without need of conscious thought or planning, the only emotion in my mind was the remembrance of playing this very song at Trumpet Man's funeral so many years ago. The more I reminisced, the more I let myself go, losing track of where I was and with whom. Seeing the red glow of the spotlights behind my tightly closed eyelids, I could visualize Trumpet Man's casket before Cassie's tear-soaked face in the front row. My funereal and soulful rendition of this song took absolute command of my senses as the tears started to roll down my cheeks.

My mind wandered to thoughts about The Performer and the Williamsburg clan, and I realized that I was once again experiencing the now familiar sensation of simultaneously thinking about the music I was playing, and my reaction to it. Lost in the moment, I felt myself *rising* from the confines of my physical body on stage, a feeling that was becoming so comforting and welcoming. I knew I was on my way to The Zone. Exactly as had happened in Williamsport only a short week ago, I felt a violent tug on my mind, intuiting Violetta's heartbreaking plea.

'Don't leave me alone, Woody…take me with you.'

As before, I held out my thoughts as if a rope for her to grab onto, despite suspecting in my soul that Violetta would not be traveling with me this night. At that precise moment of realization, I heard the familiar voice of Trumpet Man with a whisper of cold air in my ear.

'Hey, kid…'

For reasons I'll never understand I reacted to his appearance in a panic, as I had done on that first journey so many years ago. Why should that be? After all, I had become a regular traveler to The Zone, where I had communicated with Trumpet Man in the vestibule and with others beyond the inner doors. There was a sudden flash of brilliant white light. I looked down to the stage below to see Violetta following my ascent with her eyes, one hand actually raised in a desperate physical gesture of trying to grab onto me. And I saw myself, floating above the concert hall, observing the audience not at all confused by my ascent, since that rising was beyond the scope of their worldly senses. And still I saw Violetta's hand being lifted and held in the air in mid-song. The last thing I remember seeing was Lenny Dee's gaze following my ascension from far below. Last night, his arthritic fingers were steepled to his lips in the sheer joy of observing our ascent, as if knowing where we were destined to travel. But tonight, the terror was evident in his strained expression as he saw me catapulted into deep space from a pinpoint location on earth, as if sling-shot through a wormhole into another dimension.

I experienced the horrific realization that I couldn't hear anything. Oh, I could see everything receding into the distance, looking smaller and smaller by the moment below me, but there was no sound, as if sucked from my mind by a giant vacuum. I knew then that I was about to confront a ghastly twist in my fate, for I was floating, totally alone, without direction, without Violetta, without Trumpet Man, and without my music to guide me.

'Oh, Violetta, I can see this is gonna be a funny evening.'

# Chapter Four

*Violetta*

The last thing I clearly remembered was the sight of Woody *rising* from the confines of his physical body. His beautiful and bright aura floated up gently towards the ceiling of the Ellicott Club, drifting as if without a care or concern for worldly matters. Whether from the shock of the realization that he was traveling without me, or from the surprise that he had somehow overcome the negativity of the beginning of our evening performance, I couldn't say. Despite my false and forced attempt at using "Stardust" to escape my worldly bonds, Woody had somehow managed to overcome all my faults, undoubtedly by focusing his energy totally on the music and his playing, whereupon he began his much-deserved ascent.

I should have known better. As Woody had confided to me earlier the advice he had received from Trumpet Man about traveling to The Zone, *'either you get there on your own, for the right reasons, at the right time, in the right way, or you don't get there at all.'* But as I sat there, watching him escape the pain I was feeling at that moment, I couldn't help myself. Selfishly, I reached out to him, first with my eyes, then with my hand, hoping against all hope that he could pull me up with him. I knew this was wrong. And I knew it couldn't happen that way, for I had done everything possible on this evening to guarantee that I would be bound to this stage as if with a ball and chain. But I reached out for him anyway, and I saw his eyes desperately meeting my gaze, trying against all odds to help me, but to no avail. That's when I was overwhelmed by a brilliant flash of white light, convinced a nuclear explosion had rocked our world and would change it forever. At that moment, I saw Woody being thrust outward at remarkable speed, disappearing from my view in that flash of an instant, and I feared he was lost to me forever.

I sat there, feeling so totally desperate on that stage, unable to do anything but reach out to him. But he was gone. And I was alone once more. I have no recollection of anything else. I'm told that I would be dead if not for Lenny. I lay here in this bed, stunned at the ability of this arthritic little man to lift me in his arms and carry me to safety, risking his own life in the process. Indeed, he *did* give his own life to save mine. This strange little man, my guardian, whom many viewed as a buffoon, was nothing less than a hero, saving my life for a second time. Through my tears, I prayed that he would in the end be reunited with my parents, for the three of them shared a love and trust that transcends all else.

When I awoke yesterday in this bed, arms and hands heavily bandaged in white, I opened my eyes in confusion, thinking that I was awakening after the car crash that had claimed my parents' lives those years ago. My mind took me back in time, reminding me of my loss and my torment. It took me several hours to realize that this was not that time, but a new time, years having passed in between. The bandages were heaviest on my hands. I wondered, selfishly, if I would ever play the guitar again. Imagine, my life being saved by Lenny sacrificing his, and me thinking only about myself. I felt shame on top of my pain and fear. The doctor told me I would require several months of painful and plodding rehabilitation before I could hope to achieve use of my hands, and then there was no guarantee I would regain my former facility on guitar. Having already endured a long rehabilitation in my otherwise short life, my first thought was to give up the battle before it even began. But then I envisioned Woody's eyes holding mine, willing me to never give up hope of recovery and finding each other once again. And how unfair it would have been to Lenny for me to give up so easily. He never did. If nothing else, I owed him my best effort at life.

How strange that I would have walled myself off for such a long time, only to fall in love with Woody at first sight. How could I ever forget that first time I saw him sitting at his table in the restaurant of the Williamsport hotel, looking at me like a love-struck teenager? In truth, I knew at that very first moment that something else was at work, drawing us together for reasons neither of us could comprehend at that time. I shocked myself first by accepting his invitation to join him at his table on my break between sets. Despite all too many invitations by young and old men alike prior to Woody, I had never said '*yes, thank you,*' preferring instead to shield myself from all human contact for fear of feeling anything close to joy or happiness. But when Woody asked me, it felt so natural to let go and share even a little of myself with him. Who could have predicted that I would go so far as to invite him to perform with me for my final set that evening? Since losing my parents, I had never invited another musician to share my feelings, let alone my stage! In truth, I had no idea if he could even play. For all I knew, he could have been a first-year music student still practicing a C-major scale for hours on end. But as he told me about his performances earlier that week in Williamsburg, his eyes told me that he was much more than I could have imagined, indeed, hoped for.

I'll always remember starting out my last set that evening, our first set together, with "Lush Life." Yes, I knew it was a mean trick. I should have cut him some slack and played "Misty," or something just as easy and well known to all. I admit to a certain degree of selfishness. To this day, I can't be sure if I began with "Lush Life" to challenge him, or to humiliate him. It was shameful that I would have put him on the spot like that without even a hint of a warning. But when he eased in with that beautiful and soulful tenor sax of his, so gently and compassionately weaving his musical answers around my musical questions, I was overcome with a feeling of warmth I had never experienced before. If you must know, it felt like we were making love right there on that little stage in front of anyone who cared to watch! I've heard it said that the first time is always special, but nothing could have prepared me for what I felt that night. And when I gave the stage over to him during the second chorus, how he soared above it all like a majestic eagle riding the air currents! At that moment, I knew we were destined to be together forever. Or so I thought.

I lie here, still, wondering where he is, what has happened to him, for no one can recall seeing him escape the fire that claimed Lenny and his treasured Ellicott Club that evening. The most I can do now is think of Woody, and try my best to communicate with him at least in thought as I did on our first travels to The Zone.

*'Woody…come back to me…please…'*

# Chapter Five

*Lenny Dee*

Nuttin' felt right about Sat'rday night. I knew it, soon as my little flower walked in wit da kid, late and rushed like dat. What's'a madder wit kids dese days, anyway? Don't dey know how short life is, how tough to catch a break?

Last night, now dat was anodder story! Dey were great! Ohhh, when I saw dem go up t'gedder, up into da light, I just knew where dey was headed. I stood dere, watchin' 'em float, wishin' I could go wid 'em. I never could forget da first time I met her folks, years ago. Boy, dey were somp'in special, I tell ya. And when Violetta's daddy asked me to watch over her if anyt'ing ever happened to dem, I was in shock. Nobody nev'r asked me to do somp'in so 'mportant before. And when dey died in dat car crash, I knew I had to honor my word and take good care of Violetta. An' dat's what I done. I visit her whenever I could. I call 'er on da phone ev'ry day. I never let 'er give up hope. After all, a promise ain't somp'in to take lightly. I gave my word. And I was gonna keep it, no matter what. Besides, if I was ever lucky 'nough to have my own kid, I would'a wanted her to be jus' like Violetta…tough, and beautiful, not to mention talented! What a sweet kid.

Ohhh, geez, when she waltzed in here Friday night with da kid, I figured we was in for some real trouble! But it did'n take me long to see he was a real good boy. I could see da love in his eyes wid'out even lookin'. Dese two kids belonged togedder, I knew dat right away. An' I knew Violetta's parents would love 'im, 'cuz *she* sure did! But when all hell broke loose Sat'rday night, I knew we was in for a bad time. Da place was burnin' down 'round us, and Violetta, she's just sittin' dere on da stage, lookin' up, reachin' for Woody. I knew he was a'ready gone. I saw 'im floatin' up, reachin' back for 'er, but it was too late for 'im to help. So I knew I had to be da one to save my little girl from harm. I ran up to da stage as fast as my little legs would carry me. Violetta did'n even see or hear me. She just kept lookin' up, reachin' for Woody. So I grabbed 'er, picked 'er up in my arms, an' carried 'er out t'rough the smoke and flames. Da place was collapsin' all 'round us, but I never stopped, never quit. I had made a solemn promise, after all, an' I would'n go back on my word, just like I never broke my promise to my other sweet little flower.

By da time I got us outside, I gotta tell 'ya, I was feelin' pretty sick, 'ya know? My chest was feelin' real tight, like I could'n breathe. I r'member, dose fireman had to pry Violetta outa my arms. I finally let go, I guess, 'cuz I was layin' dere, watchin' dose boys put 'er on a stretcher and load 'er onto dat amb'lance. Between youse and me, I knew I was a gonner by den. Ohhhh, dey put da mask over my face, but I knew it was too late for me. The last t'ing I r'member is seein' my Violetta's face, and the face of my other flower right next to her, so close I could almost touch 'em both. So I guess I just let go. I knew I dun my duty and save my Violetta. I just prayed dose last few minutes, hopin' I would see both der parents again, wherever dey were…'cuz I was on my way dere, too. I closed my eyes. An' ya know what? It did'n hurt, not even a little. No, it felt real warm and peaceful. So I let go.

# Chapter Six

*Woody*

Without a conscious thought of time passing, I found myself back on stage, back in the moment, down on my knees gasping for breath, soaking up the thunderous applause from the audience. I could sense the shocked looks of disbelief on the faces of the musicians behind me as I turned my head to salvage my bearings. The standing ovation continued, the crowd now realizing they had witnessed something they would likely never see or hear again in this lifetime. I slowly got to my feet, exhausted from the experience. It was all I could do to drag my body off-stage, where I collapsed onto the floor, barely managing to keep my sax from crushing damage. Thankfully, the curtains drew to a close, and the show was over. The other musicians came running off the stage towards me, concern in their eyes as they saw me sprawled on the floor, saxophone cradled protectively on my chest.

The first to reach me was the bass player, he a bald-headed giant named Armstrong Fingers. It was all I could do to gather enough strength to ask him what had just happened.

"*Mannnn*, Woody, you were *wayyyy* out there *this* time!"

With that, Armstrong helped me to my feet, and half-carried me into the dressing room for a few moments of much needed rest. It took all my strength to keep my weary eyes from closing. As I relented without choice to the deep sleep, something didn't feel right. Indeed, something felt very wrong, just beyond the grasp of my mind as it prepared for shutdown moments from now. If only I could focus…

The next thing I remember was waking from a dream, totally unaware of where I was, how I got there, and how long I'd been there. As I opened my eyes, I could see Armstrong, looking intently at me from a chair nearby. I sat up slowly, realizing that I was on a couch, with a pillow and blanket at my head and feet. I felt myself staring into his eyes, recognizing a face I had known for at least 25 years, yet unable to call to my mind anything about this man who was obviously both friend and colleague.

"Welcome back, Woody," he said tentatively.

"Armstrong…where am I?" I asked in a hoarse whisper.

"Where do you think? Like always, you're in my pad, sleepin' on my couch," he answered, with the hint of a smile slowly forming. He raised one eyebrow before uttering his next words. "You were gone on a long trip this time, Woody. I've *never* heard you play like you did last night. Straight out of a dream, it was."

"Or a nightmare," I added without thought as I looked at him vacuously. My only recollection was being helped into the dressing room after last night's show, of which I could remember nothing. Here I was, a fifty-six year-old man, yet again strung out from my travels to otherworldly places so few could even contemplate, let alone understand, yet again waking on a couch in someone else's apartment, trying to focus on what had just happened to me. I couldn't shake the feeling I had. Nothing fit in this picture, including me. I was a man in the wrong place at the wrong time, unable to touch the reality of the moment. I stood slowly, the blanket still draped around my shoulders.

"Go ahead, grab a shower and a shave," Armstrong kidded. "I'll fix us a good lunch."

"What happened to breakfast?" I asked, looking back at him from the doorway to the bathroom.

"Breakfast? Afraid you slept through that meal, Woody," he mused with shaking head.

A long hot shower did wonders for my mind and body. Feeling not only revitalized but also ravenously hungry, I threw on the clothes Armstrong had thoughtfully left neatly stacked atop the closed toilet seat. True to form, he had tossed my dirty clothes from last night into a laundry bag, which I picked up and placed near the door. I joined him at his kitchen table for a familiar lunch of grilled cheese sandwiches and pasta salad with a dose of strong java to get the mind working again.

"Woody, I gotta tell ya," Armstrong began, shaking his head once again in disbelief. "In the 25 years we've been playing together in this band, I've *never* heard you play like you did last night. It was truly inspirational, my man!"

"If only I could remember it," I answered. "But once the spirit overtakes me...sorry for the pun...I have no memory of playing a note. It's kind of a Catch-22, you know? You work so hard to achieve the moment, you take off, and then...*poof*...you're off to somewhere else in the flicker of an eyelid."

"Woody, you're truly blessed," Armstrong continued between bites. "Do you have any idea how many of us try as we will to travel with you? Yet we never seem to get there. Why is that?"

"Be careful what you wish for, Armstrong," I chided.

After a few minutes of uncomfortable silence, he leaned back in his chair, lacing his huge hands behind his thick neck.

"What's the matter, Woody? You don't seem like yourself today," he said.

I took a long swig of coffee before answering.

"Oh, I don't know, Armstrong. Something just feels...you know...*wrong*. Maybe out of place. I can't really explain it, but I feel like I'm somewhere I'm not supposed to be."

"You *are* somewhere you're not supposed to be," he laughed loudly, his freshly shaved head nodding vigorously with the words. "You're in my apartment after a gig again, instead of being in your own pad with someone far better lookin' than me!"

I looked at him intensely, grateful for his years of friendship before answering.

"Yeah, you're right, big man. Time for me to vanish."

With that, I got up to leave. Armstrong just sat there, his hands still behind his head as he leaned his chair against the wall behind him. Then he reached out one of his big paws to initiate the parting handshake that had become so comfortable for us over the years. Taking his hand, I was reminded how appropriate the name Armstrong Fingers was for this gentle giant of a man. I was lucky to have him as a friend.

"Good thing for you, we've got a few nights off before our next gig. See you then," he concluded as I left with my sax case in one hand and laundry bag in the other.

I walked outside to a cold and dismal afternoon, snow covering the ground from last night's downfall. A thought of snow glowing in the streetlights brought on an unexpected feeling of déjà vu that I couldn't quite put my finger on. The more I reached for it, the farther it receded from my grasp. I opened my car door to the realization that I couldn't have driven here last night. Maybe one of the other band mates had followed Armstrong home in my car to help out. Regardless, I started the car, pulled away from the curb, and there it was again. Nothing I could grab onto, just a feeling that I had already experienced this moment.

I drove back to my apartment and spent the next few hours tidying up a bit, chastising myself for leaving the kitchen such a mess. There it was again. This time, it was the rather insane notion that my kitchen had been spotless before I left. What was happening here? I couldn't fathom an explanation for my thoughts. At about 7 p.m. I decided to go out to eat, not eager to spend my night alone in the apartment. I pulled up to the Frog Pond, one of my favorite places, only to find an hour-long wait for a table, so I left my name with the hostess and spent some time window shopping along Park Avenue. I had grown up not far from here, near Cobbs Hill, and was grateful that the neighborhood hadn't changed much since my youth. Same buildings. Different names.

45 minutes later, I was back where I started, and it's a good thing, for my table had just opened up a few minutes early, so I grabbed it gratefully, hunger once again getting the better of me. The waitress greeted me with a smile and mischief in her eyes as she spoke.

"Hi Woody," she said. "I haven't seen you in a while. You been on the road again?"

"Oh, Hi Briggett," I answered. "Yeah, as a matter of fact..."

That's as far as I got before the feeling overtook me again. Briggett's smile quickly faded, replaced by a look of concern over my well being as I sat there frozen in mid-sentence.

"Woody...are you all right?" she asked as if fearing the answer. "You look like you've seen a ghost."

I stared at her long and hard before mustering the will to answer.

"Briggett...why do I have the insane feeling that you already asked me that very same question?"

She actually took a step back, convinced something dreadful was about to happen.

"Woody...I haven't seen you for months," she said softly and slowly, making certain I understood each and every word.

"Are you sure?" I asked stupidly.

"Of course I'm sure. Are you...*on* something, Woody?"

"No, don't be silly, Briggett. You know me better than that. It's just...well...I can't shake the feeling that you asked me that same question last night."

"First of all, Woody, you weren't in here last night. Second of all, you're scaring me to death. Did something happen to you?"

By now fully ashamed and embarrassed, I threw my arms up in the air in surrender.

"Aww, I'm sorry, Briggett. I'm okay. Really, I am. It's just been a strange day. I think what I need about now is a heaping stack of oat pancakes, heavy on the maple syrup, light on the butter, please."

There it was again. I decided not to alarm Briggett any more than I already had, so I kept this thought to myself. She left to deliver my order to the kitchen, looking back over her shoulder suspiciously to see if I was about to do anything crazy, I guess. But it *was* crazy. No matter how hard I tried, I couldn't grab onto what was bothering me. Nothing fit. Nothing felt right or...normal, for want of a better word.

I drove back to my apartment as soon as I wolfed down the oat pancakes, nagged the whole way by the feeling that I was supposed to do something today and by not doing it I'd regret it later. What was I supposed to do today? It was Sunday, after all, a coveted day of rest after a long week of gigs. I parked the car and hauled my sax and laundry upstairs to my apartment. I had lived here for longer than I cared to admit. But I always felt comfortable in this place. About ten years ago I decided to buy the building when it came on the market for sale. I couldn't bear the thought of leaving what had become my home, so I kept the apartment for myself, fixed it up, and rented the three other apartments out to people I knew and trusted. It provided a steady revenue stream for me that I had never known before, and allowed me the freedom of living where I wanted, coming and going as I chose to. It also gave me an education in the advantages of owning real estate, even with the unavoidable problems associated with the constant maintenance require-ments of my renters' needs.

I plunked myself down in the chair in front of the TV to catch up on some news before going to bed. It must have been a slow news day, as Sundays often are, because I nodded off to sleep within twenty minutes, my head lolling back onto the pillow propped behind me. I recall being in that moment in time when you know you're dreaming, because your very awareness of the dreaming process means you're about to wake up. I figured I had a minute or two remaining to dream, so I let it roll. In my dream, I saw myself as if from above, walking down Park Avenue with my arm around the shoulder of a woman whose face I couldn't see. It was snowing, the heavy flakes glowing in the warmth of the streetlights. She was laughing. She put her arm around my waist from behind as we walked and then...and then I woke up.

# Chapter Seven

I opened my eyes to see pretty much the same news program I had fallen asleep watching. I guess MSNBC just keeps repeating the same segments throughout the night without worrying about boring sleeping viewers. I turned off the tube and went to bed in the hope of rejoining my dream where it had left off. Such was not to be the case, at least on this night. The harder I tried to fall asleep, the wider awake I became, until I finally gave up around 6 a.m. Exhausted from lack of sleep but too wired to feel tired, I took a long hot shower before going out for breakfast. I decided against returning to The Toad Lagoon, unsure how welcome I'd be after my odd behavior last night. I ended up at a little bagel and coffee shop around the corner from my apartment, where I spent the better part of the morning trying to figure out what was going on in my life. People came and went around me, nobody except the owner noticing that I stayed and stayed for want of a better place to sit and think. I must have been quite the topic of owner-to-wife conversation when I finally left.

I decided to drive over to Armstrong's pad around 10:30. It took a half dozen or more loud knocks to wake him at this ungodly hour for most musicians. I was about to turn around and leave when he opened the door, his eyes squinting from the light outside.

"Woody...what are *you* doin' here?" he asked in a fog.

"Armstrong...I need to talk. I've been up all night thinking," I answered.

"Man...what time *is* it, anyway?"

"It's late...around 10:45," I smiled.

"A.M. or P.M.," he snarled.

"Oops...I guess I'm about twelve hours early, huh?"

I knew he would lighten up and invite me in, which he did, turning to walk into his living room without need of formally asking me to enter his sanctuary.

"Brew some coffee," he commanded. "I'll be dressed in a minute."

I had pretty much overdosed on caffeine already, but I knew *he'd* need some to get his brain in gear. By the time I had his cup filled and on the table he stumbled into the kitchen, one hand stroking the dark stubble showing on his as yet unshaved head. He plopped down in his chair, slapped his face a few times in a comedic show of waking himself up, and took a rescuing swig of his coffee before speaking.

"Okay," he began. "I'm awake, like it or not. What's up?"

I paused, my hands around the cup I had poured for myself more as a gesture of camaraderie than for need of a jolt, gathering my thoughts.

"What happened last night, Armstrong?"

"What do you mean, 'what happened last night'?"

"I mean, tell me about the gig," I coached.

"What do you wanna know, Woody?"

"Tell me about what happened when I...left," I wondered. "What song were we playing?"

He scratched his head while making a show of looking up at the ceiling to refresh his recollection of the previous evening.

"Well, Bennie called out that Chicago blues-style arrangement of 'Stardust' you like so much. Strange thing is, you didn't even wait for him to finish the intro, Woody. You just jumped right in over top of his singing…kind of surprised us all. You know how you normally take your time to build through your solo?"

"Yeah," I nodded, searching for any answer.

"Well, last night was different. It was like you were on a mission or something. Man, you just took off into the stratosphere, right off the bat. Notes were flyin' out of your sax faster than I've ever heard before, Woody. After about ten minutes or so, I knew you'd gone off to wherever it is you go, because we all stopped playin' and you just kept on wailin' as if we weren't even there any more. The audience was goin' crazy, stompin' their feet, screamin' louder with every note you played, as if they couldn't get enough of it. When the time seemed right, we all just kicked back in, figurin' you were about ready to collapse. Sure enough, you were soon down on your knees, gaspin' for one more breath, like you always do."

"Then what happened, Armstrong?"

"Then you hauled your sorry little butt off stage and collapsed in a heap. The show was over, the curtains closed, and I carried you into the dressing room, where you zoned out like a dead man. I brought you here in my car. Bennie followed with your car, left it at my place, and got a ride home with Herbie. And here you are…*again*."

"Okay, okay…but…did anything…*strange*…happen last night, Armstrong?"

He looked at me long and hard before his face lit up, the laughter overtaking him.

51

"Strange? Woody, every time we play," he said, shaking his head in disbelief at the absurdity of my question, "you get stranger and stranger! And you ask me if anything was *strange?* Gimme me a *break,* man! You're the strangest dude I know!"

"I know, I know," I conceded, "but I never left the stage, did I?"

Armstrong thought for a long moment before answering.

"Let's put it this way," he said. "Your *body* never left the stage. Where your *mind* went, only *you* know! End of story."

I got up to leave, patting him on the shoulder as I took my cup over to the sink.

"Aren't you even gonna drink your coffee?" he asked.

"Naw...I'm too wired already, man."

"Well, don't dump it out. I'll drink it. I hate to waste a perfectly good cup of coffee," he lamented.

"Thanks, Armstrong. You're a good friend...no matter what anyone else says," I joked on my way out the door.

"I must be," he called out to my back. "Who else would put up with your *strangeness?*"

I spent the rest of the day just driving around, trying to figure out the significance of anything and everything Armstrong had said. There was a thread there, I knew, but I couldn't grasp it. As always, the more you reach, the further it recedes.

# Chapter Eight

Monday night was a carbon copy of Sunday night. I sat in front of the TV and watched the news, fell asleep, and grabbed onto that moment of consciousness just before you're about to wake up from the dream you're immersed in. This time, I was on stage performing. I could only see *myself* in the dream as I started to rise out of body during "Stardust," as so often happens these days when I play that song. But something was wrong, because in my dream I could feel the pull on my thoughts, sensing the panic in the two emerald green eyes I looked down into from above. I suspect those eyes belonged to the same girl I saw myself walking with in my dream last night. Although I couldn't see her face clearly, I saw those eyes, as she seemed to reach out for me, the distance between us quickly growing, until I couldn't see her at all anymore. There was a flash of brilliant white light and then...and then I woke up.

The rest of the week progressed pretty much according to the same script. Each night, I came closer to seeing the same girl. One time, it was in a booth at the Toad Lagoon, and Briggett was there, asking me where I'd been for so long. Another time it was in the car, and the same girl was unlocking my car door from the inside, teasing me about something. And each time, I seemed to wake up before I could see her face or figure out who she was and how she fit into my life. With each new dream I seemed to get a little closer to figuring it all out. But as soon as I woke up, her image receded further and further into my subconscious, to the point where I found myself looking forward to going to sleep in front of the TV, knowing I'd feel her presence again.

By Thursday I was pretty much wasted from lack of sleep. I was scheduled to perform with the band Friday and Saturday nights, so after breakfast I took my gig clothes out of Armstrong's laundry bag and headed out to the cleaners.

"Hey, Mr. Reed!" boomed Oscar from behind the counter.

"Hi, Oscar. How ya' been?"

"Oh, I can't complain. Nobody will listen anyway!"

"Ain't it the truth!" I chuckled.

As we were talking, he checked the pants I'd dumped on the counter to make sure I hadn't left anything in the pockets before throwing them into the hamper. But this time, unlike the hundreds of other times I'd gone through this same ritual with Oscar, he pulled a wad of money out of my to-be-cleaned pants.

"Whoa, Mr. Reed," he admonished loudly. "You've been coming here for years, and this is the first time I ever found anything in your pockets. It's a good thing I checked!"

He took pride in handing over the money that was stuffed into the pocket. I was stunned. Not wanting to make a scene or admit my lack of knowledge about where that money could have come from, I just smiled gratefully and thanked Oscar for being so honest. I didn't look at the wad of money until I got into my car, making sure no one was watching me as I sat there peeling off two hundred-dollar bills wrapped around a hand-written note.

Violetta was right.
I ain't never heard anyone play so good as you.
Her Mama & Papa must love you…
See you tomorrow night, kid.
Lenny Dee

I read the note again and again before it dawned on me that Violetta must be the girl in my dreams. No matter how hard I tried to visualize her face, all I could conjure up were two green eyes following my ascent from the stage. Is it possible I could have performed with this person and not even remembered? And if so, when? And who was Lenny Dee?

I went to sleep Thursday night in front of the tube again, searching for an answer. In the moment before I knew I would wake from this dream, I saw myself with Violetta again. But this time, I seemed to be looking at myself in a mirror, as if I was a third party observing the scene being played out in front of my eyes. I was startled out of my reverie by the realization that in my dream I was…well…younger…*much* younger than I am now, with not a trace of gray hair, and curls much longer than the style of today. It's as if I was looking back over my life through a set of binoculars, with the big lenses placed up against my eyes instead of the small ones, looking back through time with an oddly distorted vision.

But this night, I didn't wake up. I remained asleep in front of the TV, oblivious to the world, offering me no further hints at what and whom I had seen in my dream. By the time I awoke that morning at 7:30, I was already exhausted from my unwelcome nightly ritual of searching for answers that didn't seem ready to reveal themselves.

# Chapter Nine

*Violetta*

I lay in that hospital bed for weeks, searching for Woody in my dreams. It was getting harder and harder to call up his face in my mind's eye. I just knew that I had to find him. And I sensed that he would be doing the same for me, if he were still alive. I refused to believe that he had died in the fire. But if not, something drastic must have happened to keep him from visiting me. Of that I had no doubt.

I was finally released from the hospital, suddenly aware that I was once again totally alone in this world, with neither friend nor home to go back to. Even my most precious possession, my guitar, had perished in the fire. And then it hit me. I had left my bus at Woody's apartment that night, hadn't I? Yes, we had agreed we would spend the weekend at his apartment before taking to the road together in my bus for our next gigs. On the spur of the moment, I hailed a taxi in front of the hospital and gave the driver Woody's address. Within minutes, as we pulled up to the apartment building I remembered as if from a dream, my heart started beating wildly, for there, in Woody's parking space, was my bus! I jumped out of the cab before it had even come to a complete stop, barely remembering to pay the driver. As he sped away, I reached into the meager little bag I was handed by the hospital nurse, representing what was left of my life. My knees buckled when I found my keys in the bottom of the bag, first by sound, then by touch. Despite my lame leg, I virtually ran to the bus, inserted the key, whereupon the door swung open to welcome me home. Everything was exactly where I had left it. So, at least I hadn't lost my home after all! Thank you Lord, for all blessings.

I took only a moment to gather my thoughts before hurrying up the stairs to Woody's apartment. I knocked...and knocked...and knocked, louder each time. A sense of dread overtook me with each unanswered knock. Out of the corner of my eye, I saw someone approaching me in the hallway from the floor above.

"Excuse me...can I help you?" he asked gently.

"I'm looking for Woody...Woody Reed," I answered with the sound of desperation obvious in my shaking voice.

He looked at me for what seemed like minutes before asking, "Are you a friend of Woody's?"

I wanted to scream at the stupidity of his question, but I calmed myself before answering, simply, "Yes."

Again, he paused too long before finally answering me.

"We haven't seen Woody since...the fire," he hesitated.

"At the Ellicott Club?" I burst out.

"You were there?" he queried.

"Yes, I was there. Woody and I performed together that night and...and I need to find him."

I saw him looking down at my hands, still red from the burns I had spent the past many weeks trying to heal.

"I wish I could help you," he said with genuine compassion, "but no one has seen or heard from Woody since that night. For all anybody knows, he could have..."

He stopped short, not wanting or unable to finish his sentence. Undaunted, I asked him if he would jot down the phone number for my bus phone and give it to Woody when he returned home, refusing to admit that he might never do so. Under the phone number I wrote a short note:

*Woody...call me...Violetta.*

"Violetta?" he asked as he glanced at what I had written before folding the note into his shirt pocket.

"Yes...Violetta."

"I will tell him, Violetta. I promise."

With that, he slowly turned and walked back up the stairs to his own apartment.

# Chapter Ten

*Briggett*

As soon as she walked in the door, I knew I had seen or met her before. But I couldn't place her right away. You know how it is. When you wait tables at a place like the Frog Pond, you meet dozens of new people every week. It's pretty hard to keep track of who everyone is after a while. She made a point of waiting until a table opened up in my section before she took a seat, alone, looking like a lost soul. I knew right away that I had seen those green eyes before, but in a different context. I approached her quickly, handing her a menu, when she spoke to me with a shaky voice.

"Hi, Briggett," she offered hesitantly.

"Hi! How are *you* tonight?" I asked as if I had known her for years. But she wasn't fooled. Not even for a moment.

"You don't remember me, do you?" she asked, unable to mask the look of desperation so evident on her face.

I stared at her for an instant before deciding to answer as honestly as I could.

"I'm sorry, but…no, I don't remember you. Well, actually, I know I've seen you before, but I'm afraid I can't remember where or when," I said.

"That's all right," she offered with a thoughtful half-smile. "Why would you, anyway?"

And in that moment it came to me! She was the girl who had come in here to eat with Woody Reed the last time I had seen him.

"Wait a minute, *now* I remember!" I blurted out with a loud laugh. "You came in here with Woody Reed, didn't you? Let's see…is your name *Valerie*? No, wait…oh, I know it starts with a V," I stammered clumsily, fingers to my lips.

No sooner had I uttered those words than her face became even darker, as if she were about to cry.

"So…you haven't seen Woody since then?" she almost pleaded.

"Well…now that you mention it…no, I haven't," I answered slowly. "Is something…wrong? Has something happened?"

"I don't know, Briggett…but I need to find him. He seems to have dropped off the face of the earth."

"*Now* I remember. It's Violetta, *isn't* it?" I asked after snapping my fingers in recognition.

"You have a good memory," she said with glittering eyes that forewarned of tears about to flow.

"Listen, Violetta, I can't really talk right now, we're kind of busy, as you can see. But how about if you wait 'til I'm off at the end of the night, and we can talk then, for as long as you'd like. In fact, I wouldn't mind the company if you'd care to come over to my place and share some coffee and conversation. What do you say?"

"I'd like that, Briggett. And…thank you."

"Great! In the meantime, I'll bet you could use a good dinner. And I'll bet I know exactly what you'd like," I joked knowingly.

She tilted her head, wondering what I meant. Within minutes, I had returned to her table with a plateful of oat pancakes, heavy on the maple syrup, light on the butter. And that's when the tears finally broke loose. I put my arm around her shoulder, feeling like a mother taking in a stray cat.

"Later...we'll talk," I said, reluctantly returning to my other tables.

# Chapter Eleven

*Woody*

I showed up at the gig Friday night a little early and did something I usually didn't allow myself to do. I actually shared a beer or two with the guys in the band, hoping it would loosen me up. By the time we took the stage, I must confess that I was feeling a light buzz and also realizing my focus was not at all sharp. By the end of the first set, the band was cooking pretty well…all except me, that is. I just couldn't get into it. My thoughts kept drifting off to my dreams, searching for a connection to my recurrent visions of Violetta. During the break, Armstrong approached me in the dressing room with a dour look on his face.

"Come on, Woody…what's goin' on out there tonight?" he scolded.

"I don't know, Armstrong," I apologized without much conviction. "I just can't find my focus, I guess."

"Well listen, Woody. You're not doin' us much good out there, you know? So if you can't get it together for the next set, do us all a favor and sit this one out. We can't cover for you all night…and we shouldn't have to."

"You're right, you shouldn't…and you *won't* have to. I'll be fine," I tried to promise, still lacking conviction even in my own ears.

"Listen, Bennie is gonna start the next set out with 'Stardust,' okay? Just do your thing. Let it go. We'll be right behind you the whole way, Woody," he encouraged, much like a football coach spoon-feeding false emotions to his weary players before the unavoidable second half of a losing effort.

We took the stage after intermission to the hesitant applause of the audience, certainly anticipating a better closing set than the opener. Bennie immediately took the microphone in hand and began introducing the much awaited feature song of the evening, our famous Chicago blues-style rendition of that old Jazz classic, "Stardust". My eyes were glued to Bennie, trying to psyche myself out. I knew I was in deep trouble right away, because the voice I heard wasn't Bennie's, and the words coming from his mouth didn't match the movement of his lips.

"*Ladies and gentlemen,*" I heard, "*without further adieu, please welcome the Ellicott Club's own beloved artist of the guitar and voice…Violetta…accompanied this evening by brilliant tenor saxophonist Woody Reed!*"

Many in the audience had experienced my magic performance of this song before tonight, so they knew what to expect. The band kicked in with Bennie singing the introduction in his gut wrenching, gravel-voiced style. I was staring at him, yet unable to hear a thing. I looked around me to see my band mates playing. But I heard nothing. The other horn players kept shifting their gazes to me, wondering when I would decide to put my sax to my lips and join them. But I couldn't move. I was frozen in place.

Suddenly, the floodgates seemed to burst open with non-stop images and sounds. I saw an earlier time in my life, performing with Violetta, loving her and being loved in return by her. I saw Trumpet Man in the vestibule. I saw Violetta and me willing our selves through the inner door to be reunited with her parents. I saw us eating dinner at the Toad Lagoon, joking about Briggett. I saw Lenny Dee with his arthritic hands steepled in front of his face as his eyes followed our ascent to The Zone that night in the Ellicott Club. I saw The Performer on stage at the Kimball Theatre in Williamsburg, journeying to The Zone in front of my very eyes. I saw Emma Jane in her stroller as we sat on the wooden bench on the campus of the College of William and Mary, the look of wisdom in her piercing blue eyes...on and on and on the revelations continued, totally out of control. And I stood there, motionless, drowning in the torrent of emotions still beyond my comprehension.

Before I knew what was happening, the band neared the point in the arrangement where they were supposed to stop in dead silence, that being my cue to step forward to the microphone to begin my unaccompanied tenor sax solo. Herbie nudged me, pointing to the lettering on the page of music that revealed the words *Extended Tenor Solo.* He actually pushed me from behind as I continued to stand frozen, unable to respond to any stimulus. I managed to shuffle up to the microphone out of habit more than in response to his not so gentle prodding. And then the band stopped. There I stood, naked in front of the audience, unable to force my hands to move the sax to my mouth.

"Take it, Woody!" Armstrong yelled from behind.

Normally, those three words were music to my ears, giving me escape into a world I was free to create in real time. Tonight, however, those same words felt like a death sentence. The hall was silent. I looked out into a sea of expectant eyes willing me to do something...anything. Lost in a morass of conflicting thoughts and emotions, I held my sax off to the side and whispered into the microphone.

"Violetta…"

The band must have thought this was all part of some pre-planned scheme of mine, perhaps a new and unique way of entering my solo cadenza, for they seemed mesmerized along with the crowd. This time, I spoke louder.

"Violetta…please…"

You could have heard a pin drop, save for the slap echoing of my voice across the walls of the auditorium. I dropped to me knees, sax held aloft in my left hand, and I looked up to the rafters above the stage, screaming at the top of my lungs.

"Violetta…please…don't leave me alone…"

The tears were by now streaming down my face and I lowered my gaze to the floor. The concert hall remained completely silent, as if all the air had been sucked out leaving only a soundless vacuum. Everyone continued to wait for something to happen, for some clue where I was leading them in my performance, the likes of which they'd never seen or heard before tonight. Ever so slowly, I stood, turned, and walked off the stage, leaving my band mates to fend for themselves. It was only then that I could hear the murmurs begin to accost the silence. I never looked back to the stage. I didn't even put my old Conn into its velvet-lined case. I carried my sax in one hand and the case in the other right out the rear stage door into the parking lot, where I got into my car and drove off into the cold night feeling like my world had just come to a wicked and unpredictable end.

# Chapter Twelve

I drove mindlessly for several hours before the idea hit me. I needed to find the Ellicott Club, to get a handle on some connection to what was happening to me. I cleared my mind and let my memory take over the wheel, hoping it would steer me to the place where I remembered performing and ascending to The Zone with Violetta at my side. I drove for about ten minutes, feeling like a bee instinctively drawn back to the hive to deposit its honey. I arrived at the spot where the Ellicott Club had been, only to find an empty corner lot. I drove around the block several times, convinced I was in the right place. Yet each time I ended up parked in front of the same empty parcel of land. All at once overtaken by a wave of apprehension, I sped off in the direction of my apartment, not at all certain I would find it where I thought it must still stand. When I pulled my car into my parking space and saw my building, I actually started shaking from the sheer relief of the realization that I hadn't completely lost my mind…at least, not yet.

I clamored up the front steps to my apartment, only now placing my sax into its old velvet-lined case on the way through the door. Without delay, I powered up my computer and logged onto Google.com, intent on searching the city records for the

Ellicott Club. It took me more than an hour to find the last entry, a news article from the *Rochester Democrat & Chronicle* written some 25 years earlier, indicating that the club had burned down during a Saturday evening performance. According to the article, there had been only one casualty. There, in front of my eyes, I saw a picture of the club owner, Lenny Dee, eulogized as a hero for saving the life of Violetta, the headline performer, by carrying her from the burning building. The article went on to say that several members of the audience recall seeing a brilliant white flash, after which everyone fled the building in panic. According to several witnesses, Violetta had continued to sit on the stage as if in a trance, unable or unwilling to leave, looking up to the rafters with one hand raised in a gesture of reaching for something or someone. She survived only because of Lenny's heroic effort. Unfortunately, he hadn't been so lucky, collapsing on the scene as Violetta was being transported by ambulance to the hospital. The article concluded with a final mention that the building would most likely not be rebuilt, according to a reliable but unidentified spokesperson of the club.

I continued my Internet search, this time typing in *Segovia and Rostov,* for I remembered Violetta telling me the stage names of her Jazz musician parents. Sure enough, their discography and lives were well documented, supplemented by their obituaries from the violent car accident that had claimed their lives so many years ago. There was brief mention of their then 16 year-old daughter, Violetta, who had survived the crash despite massive head and leg injuries. I followed up with a search for Violetta herself, finding only a few listings of the concert career she had initiated after her long hospital recuperation. The last entry showed a program of that final weekend performing at the Ellicott Club, which indeed ended up being the final weekend for the club as well. I wasn't surprised to find no mention of me performing along side her, for my addition to the program had come at the last minute, without Lenny Dee's advance knowledge. After that last performance, Violetta seemed to have dropped off the face of the earth. I could find nothing to provide even a hint as to what fate befell her after that calamitous weekend. It was almost as if she had ceased to exist.

A soft knock on my door startled me. Looking at the clock at the bottom corner of my computer screen, I saw that it was 5:24 a.m. After a second soft knock, I got up and opened the door to find the entire band standing in my front hall, their eyes averting mine as I invited them in. They filed in soundlessly, seating themselves on the couch and floor. Armstrong was the first to speak.

"Woody…are you…all right?" he ventured, unsure of his words.

"No…I don't think I am, Armstrong," I confided sincerely. "Before anyone says anything more, I need to apologize to all of you for what happened last night. I left you guys hangin' out there all by yourselves, I know that. Frankly, I wouldn't blame you if you never spoke to me again."

They continued to quietly bore holes in my floor with their downcast eyes before Herbie, the trombonist, broke the uncomfortable silence.

"Woody…we just wanna be sure that you're all right, y'know? Something is going on with you. We sure don't know what it is, but if we can help you in any way, we will."

Armstrong picked up the flow.

"25 years of friendship doesn't get broken in one night, Woody. We just wanted you to know that," he said soothingly.

I felt like I would cry from the compassion emanating from these guys, but I was all cried out. I started speaking slowly, trying to think of the right words.

"I...don't...belong...here..." I began solemnly.

"What do you mean, '*you don't belong here,*' Woody?" Armstrong answered with a hint of annoyance in his voice.

"Listen, I need to get this out, so just open your ears. I'll start at the beginning. Please, don't say a word. Just listen first," I pleaded.

"Okay, Woody," answered Herbie. "We're all ears."

"Last Saturday night, as best I can determine, I quite literally...crash landed...onto your stage at the conclusion of '*Stardust*'. You see...I hadn't started the evening playing that song...with you..." I tried to explain.

"Woody...what are you talkin'..." Armstrong started to interject.

"Hear me out...*please!* I know how strange all this sounds, but it's certainly no stranger than anything else that's ever happened to me on my...travels. As far as I can figure at this moment, I began that performance in another time, on another stage, with another musician. I remember *rising* from my stage-bound body as I began my journey to The Zone, only to feel someone desperately attempting to pull me back. But it was too late. Suddenly, there was a flash of brilliant white light. The last thing I remember was feeling like I'd been shot out of a cannon, watching her eyes disappear below me as I rose faster than ever before. I floated, alone, high above the world...until all at once I found myself returning to the conclusion of '*Stardust*'...25 years later...with you."

Nobody said a word. After what felt like an eternity, Herbie asked the question that must have been on all their minds.

"That other musician…that was…Violetta…" he pondered aloud.

"Yes," I nodded. "Violetta."

Over the next few hours, I attempted to tell them everything I remembered about my earlier life, starting with Trumpet Man and leading all the way up to the moment in time where I now found myself. I can't say if they comprehended what they were hearing. But if they didn't, they at least allowed me the dignity to try to help me find my way. It was Armstrong who finally broke their silence.

"Woody…none of us ever pretended to know where you…traveled to…all those nights during our gigs. We've all heard tales about The Zone, knowing full well that much of what anyone says isn't from first-hand knowledge, but from legend. I think we're all willing to accept anything and everything you say to us, but I wouldn't be honest unless I admitted there's something I just can't seem to wrap my mind around," Armstrong spoke up.

"I don't blame you. All I can do is try to answer your questions," I said.

"Okay, Woody," he continued. "Let's operate on the assumption that you indeed *crash landed* on our stage, as you put it. And let's for the moment agree that we're open to the concept that you began that performance in another time, in another place, with another musician at your side. Now, assuming that we haven't all lost our minds yet by even suggesting we might be willing to believe everything you're telling us, one unanswerable question seems to remain."

I knew what was coming, but I told him to ask the question. He did.

"Just who is it that has been performing with us for the past 25 years, if not you?"

There it was, the ultimate question, for which I had not a certain answer but only conjecture.

"Believe me, Armstrong, I've spent hours trying to answer that question in my own mind!" I almost yelled. "The best I can come up with is a theory. Like any theory, it has yet to be proved true. I've told you about my journeys to The Zone, starting with the first one where I was terrified by my encounter with Trumpet Man, my mentor, and concluding with the last one, which took place last Saturday night. I've traveled to the vestibule, and finally through various inner doors that were revealed to me. Beyond those doors I experienced not just a parallel universe, but a never-ending series of parallel universes inhabited by all of us at different times and in different settings. I can't explain it any more accurately than that, because mere words don't do justice to the apparent realities that exist beyond the scope of our own physical senses. I believe with all my heart and soul that the Woody Reed you came to know over the past 25 years was me...but not *this* me," I whispered, pointing at myself as if at another person in the room.

"My theory," I continued, "is that *your* Woody Reed began his performance of 'Stardust' last Saturday night, much as I did 25 years before, and started his own ascent to The Zone, also just as I did. I believe that the flash of white light I saw that night was, for want of a better description, some kind of a cosmic shift. I was catapulted 25 years *forward,* if such a direction actually exists...and I don't think it does, if you must know...and I ended up crash landing on your stage, in this time, instead of on the stage where, when, and with whom I began."

They all sat there in total silence, contemplating the explanation I'd just offered. Bennie spoke next, doing his best to get each word out as he thought through what he'd just heard.

71

"Woody," he strained, "if what you say is true…and I don't doubt it for a moment if you say it's so…that means that…"

"Yes, Bennie," I interrupted. "That means that there's another Woody Reed out there, somewhere else, in another time, searching for these same answers in his equally unfamiliar reality, just like I am here."

"Woody, I gotta tell you," piped in Herbie, stroking his jaw and shaking his head back and forth slowly. "This is all a bit much to grasp, especially this early in the morning," he said in a feeble attempt at levity to break the ice. "But let me make sure I understand what you're saying here. If what you say is true, then all of us exist, everywhere, in all times, in all places, but without knowledge of our other selves. Is that about the gist of it?"

"Yeah…I'd say you hit the nail right on the head, Herbie," I joked.

"We all actually shared a few chuckles at the absurdity of trying to think outside the box while realizing that there *is* no box in the first place. I should have known it would be Armstrong who would speak next.

"Woody…you've got to find her!" he abruptly shouted out.

"Yes…I do," I said humbly, appreciating his empathy.

"If the Ellicott Club was the last place you were with her," he continued, "and that's no longer around, you've got to trace your steps, Woody! You're living in the wrong time, stuck in the wrong place. You've got to go back to all the places you were together, all the people you met. It's the only way…"

"I know," I whispered. "But…"

"No buts," he insisted. "Don't worry about us, or anything else for that matter. We'll survive. *You*, on the other hand, might *not* survive this, Woody."

I got up and Armstrong nearly smothered me in a bear hug, the other guys standing around us and patting me on the back encouragingly. Slowly, we untangled ourselves.

"I'm not even gonna say we'll miss you, Woody," Armstrong added as a serious afterthought. "But if your theory is correct...and I believe it is...then you...at least, the *right* you...will be rejoining us as soon as *this* you gets back to where you belong."

"That's an interesting way of saying it, Armstrong, but yeah, I believe with all my heart that's exactly what will happen...if I'm right," I said, conviction finally returning to my voice.

They solemnly departed, leaving me sitting there, on my couch, where I fell asleep within seconds from exhaustion.

# Chapter Thirteen

*Violetta*

Briggett would prove to be a true and loyal friend to me in the months to come. I waited around that first night until she finished up her shift at the Frog Pond, then followed her in my bus to her place. She owned a nice little bungalow on Vick Park A, just a few blocks from the restaurant. We stayed up all night, just talking, getting to know each other. I even got up the nerve to ask her whether she and Woody had been more than friends, although I didn't know why that should have been important to me.

"Briggett...forgive me for asking...and you don't have to answer if you don't want to, but...were you and Woody...you know..." I beat around the bush.

"Lovers?" she filled in the blank easily. "Sometimes, I wished we could have been, to be honest, Violetta. But, no, we weren't lovers. Not because I wouldn't have welcomed it, but because Woody seemed to have no interest in me as a potential bed mate. Now that I think about it, though, I believe you're the only woman I ever saw Woody with! He usually came into the restaurant alone, or with other musician friends, you know, guys in the band. But I don't think I ever saw him with another woman. Woody and I were good friends, in tune with each other but not tied to each other in any way other than friendship. In fact, Woody is probably the only male friend I've ever had!"

"I'm glad Woody has a friend like you, Briggett. And I'm glad I do, too," I confided.

"Tell me how you two met, Violetta. Maybe it'll help us come up with an answer to Woody's mysterious disappearance."

I spent the next several hours explaining to Briggett how I met and performed with Woody. I also told her that we had fallen in love at first sight. Eventually, I got around to explaining what had happened that final night at the Ellicott Club.

"That was *you?*" she gasped.

"That was me, Briggett."

"You know, I read about that in the paper, and lots of people in the restaurant were talking about it. But I don't remember seeing or hearing anything about Woody being there, or being missing! My God, for all we know, he could have...ohhh...I'm sorry, Violetta. I didn't mean to say that."

"Don't be sorry, Briggett. Just talking to you about all this is helping me more than you'll ever know. Some way, some day, I *will* find Woody. Until I do, I'll never give up hope that he's alive and well, looking for me, too."

Briggett just sat there and stared at me for at least a minute before speaking.

"You're staying *here* tonight, Violetta. No ifs, ands, or buts, young lady! And you'll stay here as long as it takes to find him!"

Much to my own surprise, I didn't argue the point. In truth, I needed a friend right then more than at any other time in my life. Briggett led me into the spare bedroom, pulled back the covers on the neatly made bed, and actually tucked me in, stroking my bangs with her finger before she turned off the light and shuffled off to her own bedroom to catch up on much needed sleep. A lifelong friendship was born, to be nourished continually and unselfishly throughout the coming years.

# Chapter Fourteen

*Woody*

After Armstrong and the guys left, I managed to sleep fitfully until about 3 o'clock that afternoon, waking up to the recollection of what I was supposed to have done last Sunday! I dialed Cassie's phone number from rediscovered memory, hoping against hope that nothing had changed in the past 25 years since missing my scheduled reunion at her house. The phone rang several times before being answered.

"Hello?" I heard a male voice answer.

"Uh…hello, is Cassie home?" I asked.

"Who?"

"Cassie…is she home?" I repeated.

"I'm sorry, you must have the wrong number," he replied. "There's no one here by that name."

He was about to hang up before I quickly asked a final question.

"I'm sorry to bother you…but, can you tell me…how long have you had this phone number, please? It's very important that I find the person who used to have this number."

He paused for a moment, unsure if I was just another telemarketer with a new line of bait-and-switch.

"Well…actually, I've had this number for about the last five or six years," he said with a hint of disdain in his voice.

Pressing my luck, I asked if he had any idea what had happened to the woman who used to have this number.

"I'm afraid I can't help you there. Now, if you don't mind, I have other matters to attend to," he concluded as he disconnected abruptly.

I shouldn't have been surprised, after all. I checked the phone book and found no listing for Cassie. I thought about Trumpet Man and Cassie's daughters, Jennifer and Jessica, but I didn't even know their married names, let alone if they even still lived in the area.

I made up my mind what I needed to do. I packed a small suitcase with the essentials and locked up the apartment, remembering to grab my saxophone at the last possible moment. I got in the car and began the drive towards Corning, New York, where Violetta had taken me to meet Mario and Maria at their downtown restaurant a little more than 25 years ago. With any luck, I would arrive there before dark, in time for dinner. The entire way there, I tried to put my thoughts in order. How does one explain 25 years of lost time? Was I losing my mind, or was I really on the right track with my theory? Assuming I was, I knew I needed to prepare myself for what I might find at every turn…a dead end. People I had known 25 years ago might have moved away, or worse, died, and I wouldn't even know it until I encountered the truth from someone along the way.

The drive gave me time to reminisce about the first time Violetta had brought me here to meet her *second family*. No sooner had Violetta and I walked through the front door 25 years ago than I heard a chorus of people calling out her name. I can hear them still, if only in my memories.

"*Violetta! Violetta!*"

It took less than three seconds for them to notice that we were holding hands before they all swooned in unison.

"*Oooohh, Violetta!*"

"*Everyone, I'd like you to meet my…friend…Woody Reed,*" she offered in introduction all those years ago.

I was suddenly surrounded by several generations of Italian accented waiters, waitresses, cooks, and bus boys, all eager to pat me on the back and make me feel welcome. In rapid succession, they fired off their names.

"*I'm Giusseppe!*"

"*I'm Mario!*"

"*I am Maria!*"

"*This is our son, Luciano!*"

"*I am the first grand-daughter, Michaellina!*"

"*This is first cousin Donnatella!*"

By the time I caught my breath, I could only stand and shake my head in disbelief.

"*I'll never remember all your names!*" I blushed. "*So, I say to you all, 'Ciao'!*"

I experienced the nagging fear that I wasn't sure if I had said 'hello' or 'good-bye,' but they didn't seem to care either way, so I stopped worrying about it as quickly as I had thought of it.

"*Ahhhh, Violetta,*" they seemed to sing in chorus.

Maria took the lead and sat us down at a table near the back as the others dispersed to attend to their assigned duties. I looked at Maria as she sat us at our table, certain that this was all a trick, and this hostess was straight from central casting for a sitcom about Italian restaurant owners in America. True to form, Maria was short, round and plump, with the traditional large white apron doing a very poor job of stretching to cover her immense breasts. Yes, her dark hair was pulled back tightly into a bun, with many strands of stray gray hair escaping to fall over her forehead into her eyes, requiring a constant swipe of the wrist to eliminate the problem. Her cheeks were soft and red, looking as if she'd just run a marathon before opening for business that day. To complete the image, she wore heavy black stockings, shuffling about in those strange open heeled and open toed black slipper-looking things you've undoubtedly always wondered about.

"We knew her Mama," Maria sang, I mean, said, looking at me but gesturing to Violetta. "And her Papa, too," this time looking directly at Violetta. "We love them both sooo much…"

Maria was obviously having a hard time fighting back the tears, so she turned and walked quickly away, leaving behind only her heartfelt sob.

"Ayyy, Mama Mia," she lamented as she waddled back to the kitchen.

Within minutes our table was loaded with every imaginable Italian pastry, heaping portions of omelets covered in marinara sauce, not to mention American-style home fried potatoes, the feast topped off with filled goblets of Mimosa. There was enough food here to feed the entire town of Corning, and we laughed together at the thought of it!

"I'll never forget the first time we came here," Violetta reminisced wistfully. "Mom and Dad were on their way to perform in Rochester, just like we are now, and they stopped in here for lunch on a day like any other. I was only about seven or eight at the time, but I can still remember that first meeting. Woody, have you ever heard the expression, 'All things happen for a reason'?"

My heart skipped a beat before I managed to answer.

"You better believe I've heard it. In fact, I feel like I've been living it for the past week!"

"Me too," she said in wonderment, peering at me as if through someone else's eyes.

It felt like everything that I experienced this week was about to culminate in a soon-to-arrive moment, although I couldn't explain why I felt that way. Violetta and I sat and stared at each other, not knowing what to say, and not wanting to lose the moment, when suddenly Maria and Mario appeared at our table, smiling broadly.

"Ahh, Violetta, we see that look before many years ago in someone else's beautiful eyes," Maria said lovingly.

Mario placed his thick hand gently on my shoulder, as if to let me know that it was all right with them that I was in love with their little girl. I turned my head back to look up at him, my expression proof that no words were needed to convey my inner feelings.

"Whenna you gonna come back again, Violetta?" Maria asked, afraid of the answer she knew she would receive.

"Soon, I hope, Maria," Violetta answered softly. "Woody and I are performing at Lenny Dee's place this weekend. Maybe on the return trip, depending on our schedule, we'll be able to stop and spend some time with you."

It took a moment to register that Lenny Dee must in fact be the Lenny that Violetta told me about the previous night at dinner. Then, all at once, Mario and Maria looked at each other incredulously, both saying the same thing at the same time.

"This boy's a musician, Violetta?"

"I'm afraid so," she said in jest. "And one of the best you'll ever hear," she added with a note of pride, boosting my frail ego immensely.

"Ayy-ayy, your Mama and Papa would be so proud of you, Violetta!"

Mario spoke to the ceiling while waving his hands back and forth in short arcs.

"If only they could be here to see you..."

They both bent down to kiss Violetta, each taking possession of a different cheek, before Mario walked over to stand beside me once more. Again, he placed his hand on my shoulder, but this time it didn't feel quite so gentle. His grip was more like an iron vise, and it was all I could do not to scream out in pain.

"Sooo…you gonna take a good care of our Violetta, yes?"

"Yes," I squeeked, not yet relenting to the fierce grip that had begun to deaden all feeling in my shoulder.

"OK, then…we gonna see you soon, no?"

"Yes," I squirmed, looking forward to getting back on the road while I still had use of my limbs.

Maria and Mario left our table, and I'm afraid my left shoulder sagged a bit at his departure, causing Violetta to laugh at the pain evident on my face.

"You didn't tell me I'd be meeting Lenny so soon!" I said, pointing a finger at her in mock anger. "So this is how you repay his kindness, by bringing me along for the ride to sit in with you at his…what…restaurant?"

"Actually, it's a lot more than a restaurant," she whispered, looking around to see if anyone was listening to our conversation, apparently about to reveal a deep, dark secret. "Lenny used to own a little dive upstate. For years, there were rumors about his connections, and eventually he opened up a very ritzy nightclub in Rochester, called The Ellicott Club. That was the only spot my parents used to play whenever they visited town. I think they just kind of hit it off with Lenny, and they built a solid following at his club. Since my rehab, I play The Ellicott one weekend every three months. Lenny may come across a little…strange…but he's really a loving person underneath the rough exterior."

"I can't wait to meet him," I said not at all convincingly. "The funny thing is, though, I can't say that I ever heard of The Ellicott Club, and I've lived in Rochester for years. And I'm sure I never heard anything about you performing in town. Had I seen your picture, you better believe I would have had a front row seat every night you were there!"

"*There you go again,*" she said with a shake of her head, still unconvinced anyone would consider her beautiful to look at. "*But I'm not surprised you never heard of the place. It's a very exclusive private music club, for members only, and they never advertise the performances to anyone but their dues-paying members. Believe me, Woody, we're talking about people with the big bucks here. Tickets for my shows go for $50 a head, and I'm on the low end of the scale!*"

"*And how big is the room?*" I wondered.

"*It seats 450 comfortably, with standing room for another 100 if needed,*" she explained.

"*Wow! That's not a room, it's a small concert hall, Violetta!*"

"*True,*" she agreed, "*and the guests aren't even seated concert style. They sit at tables of between four and ten people each, with linen table cloths and everything. Dinner and drinks are served before and after the show only, and by tuxedoed waiters, no less.*"

"*Your pal Lenny is making some serious bucks, Violetta. I hope you get a percentage of the house.*"

"*Don't I wish,*" she mused. "*But for now, I'm happy just to get my standard fee, which is still at least triple what I get anywhere else. Maybe someday...*"

"*...when you show up with a great tenor player-slash-manager!*" I jumped in.

"*You know, I think you and Lenny are going to get along just fine, Woody,*" she joked.

But her eyes hinted she was really thinking about what I'd said, despite the kidding tone of voice I had used.

"*One more thing, Woody. Lenny is very protective of me, like I was his own little girl. After the accident, he told me he had promised Dad that if anything ever happened, he would watch over me. And I must tell you he has been true to his promise. If ever I had or needed a godfather, Lenny is it! He has a tendency to come across a little, shall I say, brusque. But he has a heart of gold, especially when it comes to his precious little flower.*"

"In that case, I'm sure we'll get along famously," I said more to convince myself it was true than believing it.

"What do you say we hit the road, Woody. It's almost noon, and if we don't run into any bad weather we can be at your place by 1:30, 2:00 at the latest."

"My place?" I asked in surprise.

"I thought it might make sense to leave your car there, and pack a suitcase with anything you'll need for at least the next few weeks," she said authoritatively.

"The next few weeks?" I asked again, both eyebrows now raised.

"You did say you wanted to be the other half of my duo, didn't you?"

"Oh…yeh…absolutely," I remembered.

"And look at all the money we could save by traveling together in my bus. Why would we need two vehicles, right?"

"I have a better idea," I interrupted.

As soon as the words left my lips, though, I knew I was in for some trouble. Violetta's right eyebrow arched high, revealing a combative flicker in her eyes. Well, maybe combative is too strong a word. Let's say, argumentative. Without waiting another second, I decided to correct myself.

"What I mean is, I have another idea, Violetta. Why don't we stay in my apartment for the weekend while we're in town, then we could leave together in your bus for the rest of the trip, however long that may be?"

She looked at me pensively for a long moment, trying to decide if there was anything worth arguing about here.

"Right, then!" she agreed. "And once we leave Rochester, you can help me with the driving," she offered as the final word.

"And anything else you might need help with," I concluded with a wink, which only brought another exasperated roll of her eyes.

We said our good-byes all around the restaurant, promising to return soon. I took the lead position this time, and spent the next 90 minutes driving alone in my car, thinking back to what Trumpet

*Man had said to me about being on a mission, and returning a favor for someone he couldn't or wouldn't reveal to me. I suspected this all had something to do with Violetta, but as yet I hadn't figured out how that piece fit into the puzzle. My inner voice told me I was about to find out, like it or not.*

I finally arrived at the restaurant at around 5:45, albeit 25 years after that first visit I had just relived in my mind while driving to Corning! Despite the passage of time, the place hadn't changed all that much, other than the name on the front of the building. I slowly walked through the front door, unable to hide my disappointment at finding not a family-style Italian restaurant, but a sleek new bistro inside. A young hostess with a pierced eyebrow approached me.

"One for dinner, sir?" she asked.

"Actually," I fumbled, "I was hoping to ask you for some information first. Could you tell me what happened to the Italian restaurant that used to be here?"

"Gee, like, I never knew there *was* an Italian restaurant here," she laughed innocently.

"Is it possible I might speak with the owner for a moment?" I asked somewhat too impatiently.

"Sure…like, wait here, I'll go get 'er."

A middle-aged woman came out from behind the kitchen doors after a few minutes asking me how she could help me.

"I'm really sorry to bother you, especially at your busy dinner time," I apologized, "but I'm trying to find the people who owned the Italian restaurant that used to be here. It's really very important."

"You mean…" she prodded, attempting to see if I really knew who used to own the place.

"…Mario and Maria," I interrupted. "I'm looking for Mario and Maria."

She hesitated, looking at me long and hard before answering.

"Are you family?" she asked.

"No…just a good friend of the family," I responded.

"Well…I'm so sorry to have to tell you this," she said, taking my hand in hers gently, "but Mario and Maria passed on several years ago."

I felt the wind sucked out of my lungs and stumbled back a step or two before regaining the strength to continue my line of questioning.

"Do you know what happened to the rest of their family?"

"The last I heard, they all went back to Italy. I guess they didn't have any reason to stay, once Mario and Maria were gone."

Regaining my composure, I offered thanks for her time and concern. I left without any thought of staying for dinner, deciding instead to drive on to Williamsport, Pennsylvania, where I had first met and performed with Violetta. I refused to believe that the old downtown hotel wouldn't still be there.

# Chapter Fifteen

A couple of hours later I pulled into the lot of the old Williamsport hotel, finding that it had been turned into a Best Western. I parked my car, grabbed my suitcase and sax case, and walked into the lobby to register. As I was handed my key, I asked the clerk if they had a restaurant.

"Oh, yes, Mr. Reed," she responded eagerly. "We're very proud of our four-star restaurant."

"How late do they serve dinner?" I asked, realizing I was repeating a conversation I had had some 25 years ago.

"Until midnight. Would you like me to reserve a table for you?"

"Yes, please," I answered as I turned to find the elevator. I couldn't help but feel like this was going well, indeed a word-for-word recitation of the conversation I'd had with a different hostess in this very hotel 25 years ago on my first visit.

I rode up to my room…coincidentally, I suppose, it was a non-smoking room on the seventh floor. Entering the room, I was immediately struck by the realization this was the very same room I had stayed in 25 years ago, the first night Violetta and I had shared not only a performance but a bed! After a hot shower to revive me, I came back down to the lobby and walked towards the restaurant. The entire way, I searched for an easel with color poster at the entrance to the restaurant, remembering the first time I had seen Violetta's picture announcing her performance, held over from the weekend due to the blizzard that had shut the whole town down. While I saw no such poster, the restaurant looked pretty much the way I remembered it. The hostess greeted me as soon as I got to her welcoming podium.

"Good evening, sir. One for dinner this evening?" she asked politely.

"Yes. I have a reservation…the name is Reed," I repeated as if from a 25 year-old script.

"Ah, yes, Mr. Reed, here you are," she answered after locating my name on the reservation list. "Actually, it doesn't look you'll need a reservation tonight," she added, her previously unspoken words breaking the magic of the moment for me.

As she walked me to my table, I asked her who tonight's entertainment would be.

"I'm sorry, Mr. Reed," she answered, looking back over her shoulder at me, "but we don't have entertainment in the restaurant."

"Oh…last time I was here, they had a wonderful singer performing," I attempted to clarify before reaching my table.

"That must have been quite a long time ago, Mr. Reed," she said as I sat down. "I'm afraid they stopped booking music in here at least ten years ago."

"Ohhh…I'm sorry to hear that…" I answered, trying to hide my disappointment.

"May I get you a drink first, Mr. Reed?"

"Uhh…sure…I'll have a house ginger ale, please," I said, perhaps hoping that sticking to an old script would somehow change the present unwelcome flow of the conversation.

"Certainly," she laughed. "Thomas will be your server, Mr. Reed. He'll be with you shortly with your ginger ale and menu."

My heart stopped. The coincidence was just too much to handle. Within a few minutes, Thomas, my waiter, approached the table with my ginger ale. I wracked my brain, trying desperately to recognize him from our first meeting 25 years ago. The age seemed right...he looked to be about 50-ish or so.

"Good evening, sir," he announced as he placed my drink in front of me. "May I tell you our specials of the evening?"

"Actually," I quickly answered, "I'd like to order a plate of pasta marinara with grilled vegetables."

I could have sworn that sparked a flicker of recognition in his eyes, but I couldn't be sure, so I pressed on as he wrote my order on his pad.

"How long have you been a waiter here, Thomas?"

He smiled a weary smile as he answered.

"About 30 years, sir. Why do you ask?"

"Oh, I don't know," I said without breaking eye contact. "I remember eating here a very long time ago, when they still had entertainment. I could be wrong, but I think you might have been my waiter!"

Thomas looked at me closely and carefully before snapping his fingers in recognition.

"You're that sax player, right?"

My heart was beating a mile a minute by now.

"Man, what a memory you have!" I gushed.

"That's funny," he explained, "but as soon as you ordered pasta marinara with grilled vegetables, I *knew* I had met you before! A man *is* what he *eats*, right?"

I decided to go for broke.

"Thomas, let me ask you. Do you remember the beautiful young singer I performed with here?"

His demeanor told the story I didn't want to hear.

"Oh, what a shame that was," he said with downcast eyes. "Violetta was such a sweet person, as you surely know," he continued sadly. "The last we heard, she was burned pretty badly in a fire at some club up in Rochester the week after she left here. They took a wrecking ball to the place soon after."

"Do you know what happened to her, Thomas?"

He made a point of looking inward, searching for an answer.

"You know...we never saw or heard from her again after that. I wish I could help you more, but I just don't know what ever became of her."

"Okay...thanks, Thomas. By the way, it's good to see you again," I concluded sincerely, allowing him to turn from my table to place my order.

# Chapter Sixteen

Thinking about it, I realized that meeting Thomas could serve either to prove or debunk my theory, depending on how I looked at it. Initially, I was thrilled that he remembered me from my first performance with Violetta. Upon further thought, however, his very recollection seemed to prove my working theory wrong, in that it could be taken for proof that *this* Woody Reed…me…indeed was present in this place and in this time, albeit 25 years ago. On the other hand, it could just as easily have proved my theory correct! His recollection of hearing about the demise of the Ellicott Club and Violetta's disappearance could be taken for proof that somehow the different times and places intersected. If that was the case, it tended to lend even more credence to my belief in some sort of cosmic shift that threw our parallel universes out of kilter. Regardless of which way I looked at the problem, I wasn't about to give up and go home. There was no doubt in my mind that I would drive on to Virginia the next morning, where I would take up the search for The Performer and his Williamsburg clan.

After a sleepless night, I checked out of the hotel early, hoping to make it to Williamsburg by mid-afternoon. As soon as I pulled out of the hotel parking lot it began to snow, first lightly and then quite heavily. I experienced the déjà vu of the way I had felt when another blizzard had forced me stop here in Williamsport in the first place some 25 years ago, when and where I first met Violetta. Luckily, by the time I made it through the high terrain of Pennsylvania the snow turned to mere flakes, and I could feel the temperature rising by degrees with each hour and mile traveled.

When I finally arrived in Williamsburg hours later, I immediately drove to The Performer's house, eager to find him and seek his wise counsel. I was struck by the strange notion, however, that while 25 years had passed in a wink for me due to circumstances beyond my comprehension or control, those same years had passed at normal pace for everyone else. That meant that The Performer would now be more than 80 years old! So I shouldn't have been surprised or disappointed when the woman who answered the door told me she was sorry, but the family I was looking for had moved from here many years ago. She had no knowledge of where they might be, but as I turned to leave she suddenly remembered something.

"You know, I think I remember hearing that they decided to move back north to wherever it was they first came here from," she offered.

"Okay, thanks very much," I answered as I waved good-bye and got into my car to back out of the driveway.

My next stop was the shopping plaza where Cass and Jennifer operated their boutiques. Although the area had been heavily built up since I'd last been here, I had no trouble finding their women's store. Hoping for some good news, I entered, looking for signs of telltale blue eyes to confirm that I was indeed in the right place. I'm sure I couldn't hide my disappointment when a brown-eyed woman approached me.

"Looking for a gift for your wife, sir?" she asked.

"Actually, I'm looking for the owners," I answered.

"Oh," she said with a hint of a question in her voice. "I *am* the owner."

I told her I was looking for Cass and Jennifer, explaining that I had shopped here once before.

"Oh dear," she mused, "that must have been a long time ago! I bought this store from their family fourteen...no, fifteen years ago. They all moved back north, I think," she explained.

"And what about their kids store just a few doors down?" I asked.

She looked a little confused by my question before responding uncertainly.

"Well, I really don't know...I'm afraid I don't know anything about that..."

I thanked her for her courtesy and departed, walking three stores to the left in search of the children's boutique where I had first met Jessica and her beautiful two-and-a-half year-old daughter, Emma Jane. The store was no longer there. Wondering what my next course of action should be, I decided to drive down to Colonialand and visit the Kimball Theatre, hoping I might find a clue there. Once again, I was stunned by all the changes that had taken place over the years, which for me was only a week, after all. Despite the new buildings and roadways, it didn't take me long to locate Merchants Square, right where I remembered it being. If nothing else, the very history of this place meant that change came slowly and very little of the original town was ever replaced. Rather, it was purposefully well maintained. I left my car in a new parking garage that hadn't been here on my first visit, walking the final block or two to the Kimball Theatre.

As I approached the box office, people were milling around, looking to see what entertainment was available for the evening. Many of them were lined up to buy tickets. There was a show scheduled for 8 p.m. by a musical group called *The 3 of Us*. The picture on the marquee was small and had obviously been shot from a distance, offering little detail of the three musicians in the group. But the printed description of the band indicated they were born and raised in Williamsburg and had developed quite a reputation for excellence. I turned to leave when a funny feeling grabbed me deep down in my gut. I couldn't shake it, so I decided to go with it, whereupon I got in line and bought a ticket for the evening performance.

I had a couple of ours to kill before show time, so I took a leisurely stroll through the historic district in the direction of Shields Tavern, the very same place I had eaten before that first time I heard The Performer's show so many years ago. I was greeted by a waitress playing the role of a buxom young wench…at least I think it was only role-playing…and she served me the same meal I had enjoyed 25 years earlier, that being grilled polenta with vegetables. As before, I treated myself to a stein of stout ale and passed the time people-watching. Before I knew it, the clock chimed the half-hour after seven o'clock, so I departed the tavern and slowly walked back to the theater. I couldn't explain the combination of excitement and apprehension I was feeling. I was excited to get to hear some live music, yet apprehensive about the strange feeling I couldn't shake, as if I was once again being drawn here for reasons beyond my control.

I was ushered into the theater by an older woman whose blouse pin identified her as a volunteer. The place was filling up fast, so, as I had done years earlier, I found a seat in the middle of the auditorium, hoping for the best acoustics. Indeed, it might even have been the same seat I'd taken last week...I mean, 25 years ago. The theater hadn't changed one bit. I was comforted to see the same balcony behind me housing the sound and lighting equipment. The same heavy burgundy colored curtains graced the high, large stage. Everything was exactly as I remembered it. The pre-concert excitement was palpable, and the noisy buzz of the crowd exhilarating. As I looked around me, I couldn't help but notice that this audience was quite young, mostly college-age people of all variety, with only a handful of people over thirty. I had to remind myself that I was no longer a comparable age, but one of the few audience members who was, shall we say, old enough to be their parent and in some cases grandparent!

At 8:00 p.m., guests were still loudly filing into their seats, preventing the show from beginning on time. I was getting caught up in the fervor of waiting for these musicians to take the stage, certain I was in for a real treat if the anticipation of the rest of the audience meant anything. Finally, at 8:15, the house lights dimmed, causing a wave of raucous applause and cheers from the audience. The hair stood up on my neck, surprising me. A young man dressed in jeans and a tee shirt stepped through the curtains into the main spotlight with a microphone in hand, not bothering to try quieting the crowd for it would have been a futile effort.

"Ladies and gents," the young host shouted to be heard even with the microphone. "You don't need me to tell you why you're here tonight! So put your hands together for the best contemporary musical group ever to hail from Virginia, Williamsburg's own...*The 3 of Us!*"

With that, the audience began hooting, yelling, and stomping its feet, shaking this historic theater to its centuries-old rafters. The oversized curtains slowly opened as the stage lights were raised to full wattage, revealing an impressive array of musical instruments and electronic gadgetry covering the full breadth of the large stage. The entire center area was taken up by the biggest collection of percussion instruments I had ever seen. Gold and silver hardware glittered blindingly in the stage lights. Stage left and right were balanced with equally impressive racks of electronic keyboards and assorted guitars and violin, awaiting the evening's duty on their felt-backed stands. People began whistling loudly, eager to get this show under way.

Laser lights flashed in a dizzying array as the first member of the group virtually ran up to stage front from behind the percussion instruments. Realizing that I, too, was by now smiling broadly and emitting a few hollers of my own, I was taken aback by the obvious youth of this performer. He was, to me, but a youngster, no more than his early twenties at most. Dressed all in black, he took his bow to acknowledge the audience's applause. As he did, his thick, wavy hair fell over his forehead. Upon rising again to his full height, he brushed his hair out of his eyes with his right hand before using the same hand to wave to the audience. As soon as he looked out into the crowd, I felt locked into his piercing blue eyes, clearly visible even from this distance. He cocked his index finger and pointed right at me, as if to say '*this one's for you.*' My heart stopped in mid-beat, transporting me back in time to the first occasion I had seen The Performer on this very stage only a week…I mean, 25 years…ago. I felt myself locked into that all too familiar star-trekkian tractor beam yet again, unable to break my mind free of the strong pull. My breathing became shallow, my mind racing for an explanation of what was happening.

No sooner did he point at me than he turned around and launched himself into his percussion lair, enticing us all to follow him on an introductory trip into the rhythmic complexities of his craft. Bobbing and weaving to the powerful beats he created extemporaneously, he continued, alone, for a full five minutes or more, building in intensity, teasing the audience with only a hint of what was yet to come. Many people, unable to resist the intoxicating rhythms, stood and danced in place. Ever so slowly yet never ceasing to sway to his own beat, he eased up on his emotional outpouring as if to cue another band mate to join him on stage.

Sure enough, a beautiful young girl, for to me she was far too young to be considered a woman, bounded onto the stage to take her bow. Also dressed all in black, she looked to be about the same age as he, with deep double dimples and a long mane of golden hair pulled back into a tight pony tail which reached her thighs. Her deep, dark, mystical eyes drew me into her world. She raised both arms above her, waving to the audience almost manically, her entire body shaking back and forth with the anticipated excitement of the show yet to begin for her. Like her band mate before her, she looked out into the audience and pointed directly at me, gracing me with a wide smile and a sense of energy she couldn't hide. Just as abruptly, she turned and retreated to her place at stage left behind a rack of electronic keyboards. With a mere touch of her right index finger, she triggered what I concluded must have been the pre-programmed combination of a pumping electronic bass and snapping electric piano, by then in perfect synchronization with the driving percussion being laid forth by the young man at center stage. She reached down and picked up her electric guitar, tossing the strap over her head and shoulder in one smooth motion. And then...*she wailed!* I mean, she let loose without preamble like I'd never heard another musician emote, right down to the tips of her toes. Through it all, she never stopped smiling, making clear in no uncertain terms that she had been born to do this. She made it look so effortless, closing her eyes to focus her energies on her performance, rocking back and forth ever so gently and slowly, her unbridled smiles causing the same reaction from all who could see her. I sat mesmerized by what I was hearing, unable to stop staring at the two of them as they shared their musical gifts so unselfishly.

I knew I was in serious trouble when the third member of the trio took the stage to the thunderous applause of all in attendance. Dressed in the same uniform of all black, she ambled up to stage front as the other two musicians favored her with a fusion-rock back-beat. She had long and tight curls, framing the same piercing blue eyes she shared with the percussionist. She looked only a little older than her partners, but came across as more comfortable on stage, if that was possible. She followed their pattern of waving to the audience, then looking directly at me as if in personal welcome. Her gesture, however, included a tear rolling down one cheek as she captured my eyes with her own.

All at once, she turned and pranced across to stage right, like a ballerina, where she took up position behind her own rack of electronic gear. Joining her mates, she picked up her electric violin and proceeded to bring the house down with a cascade of improvisations hot enough to set the place on fire. In the midst of the musical frenzy, the three of them began *rising* from the confines of their physical bodies on stage. I sat in awe of what I was seeing before my eyes, for the three of them joined hands as they rose, their auras illuminating the air above the stage as they floated upward. I actually laughed out loud at the absurdity of my feelings, for this was becoming almost commonplace for me to see! Several audience members sitting in front of me turned around to glare at me, wondering what in the world would cause anyone to laugh at such a moment, despite their inability to see what I saw. As I did the first time I had seen The Performer begin his ascent, I looked around me to see if anyone but I had any idea what was taking place before their very eyes. As happened 25 years ago, no other eyes followed the ascent, for it was beyond the scope of their worldly senses. I knew I was the only person in attendance with even a clue of what was unfolding, which made me laugh all the harder.

They rose higher and higher, floating easily and without restriction above the concert hall. A rich, warm glow emanated from their path as I followed with my eyes while my ears remained fixed on their flawless and emotional performance on stage. This went on for at least ten minutes before their auras completed their journey back into their stage-bound bodies, rejoining the audience in real time. I could only wonder how long they had actually traveled, with whom they had communicated, and what the result of their journey would be. As they concluded this opening selection, they received a much-deserved standing ovation. Once settled comfortably into the groove of the evening, those in attendance took a moment to catch their collective breath, allowing the violinist the opportunity to take microphone in hand and address us soothingly.

"I can't tell you how great it is to come home again," she began sincerely. "As you know, we've been out on the road for the past year, touring this great country of ours from Pacific to Atlantic, amber waves of grain to purple mountains majesty."

The audience laughed lightly and affectionately as she continued.

"But home is where the heart is, so here we are again! Just take a look at *this* little guy," she teased while gesturing behind her towards the percussionist, actually going over and pinching his cheek to the delight of all. "Last time you saw him he still had lots of baby fat. It's funny what a year on the road will do, right?"

A chorus of appreciative cheers and whistles emanated from the female members of the audience, making it abundantly clear that this blue-eyed youngster could have his pick of groupies on this evening.

"Please put your hands together for my baby brother…Caden Michael!"

The spotlight shone on him brightly, illuminating his blushing cheeks, much to the delight of his many female admirers. He bowed deeply, once again brushing the golden hair from his eyes as he stood back up.

"Talk about babies," she gushed with a chuckle, "can you believe this babe over here? When we last performed for you she was barely out of diapers, and look at her now!"

This time, the males in the audience took over on cue, favoring the young guitarist with whistles that you might have heard in a strip joint, but not a concert hall.

"Please put your hands together," she went on, "for our cousin, Chelsea Miranda!"

Chelsea just kept smiling broadly, waving her arms at us, soaking it all in, seeming to invite the attention she was being showered with. She placed her guitar down onto its stand and bowed to her fans, her ponytail bouncing over her head from behind and hitting the floor in front of her. Giving the audience a few moments to quiet down, the violinist's verbal introduction continued more softly and earnestly than before.

"Finally, we'd like to welcome a very special guest who is seated in the audience tonight."

And then, she just stood there, staring directly into my eyes from her position at stage front. She didn't say another word. She just kept looking deep into my soul. After a few moments of this, people in the audience began looking around, trying to see who she was looking at. There were a few murmurs to be heard, but a full 30-seconds of non-stop staring left the hall soundless as all eyes returned to her on stage, seeking explanation.

"You're all too young to remember, but this person performed on this very stage 25 years ago with my Papa. Please give a warm Williamsburg welcome to a brilliant tenor saxophonist, Mr. Woody Reed."

As she said my name, her eyes demanded me to stand. In an automatic physical response to her gesture, I stood, afraid my legs wouldn't hold me for more than a moment. The next two words out of her mouth almost floored me. It was all I could do not to pass out from the shock of these words.

"Hi, Wuddy," she whispered into the microphone.

Lost in the moment, I experienced a vivid flashback to a time 25 years earlier when The Performer and I had walked across the campus of the College of William and Mary, pushing his sleeping granddaughter in her stroller. As we had sat on a wooden bench discussing my future, I recalled looking over at the two-and-a-half year old child to find her awake, her eyes fixed on me, seeming to comprehend every word that had been uttered in her presence. It was as if she possessed an inner force that suddenly had made my life decision crystal clear. I now realized that I was, once again, held captive by those same blue eyes. The young woman on stage was indeed Emma Jane.

Looking around to acknowledge polite applause by those who certainly knew nothing about me, I realized that I couldn't hear a thing. Oh, I could see their hands clapping as if in slow motion in front of my eyes, but there was absolutely no sound. I looked back up to the stage before virtually collapsing into my seat. Emma Jane continued speaking, but the movement of her lips didn't match the echo-chambered words I heard in my mind. I knew no one heard these words but me.

'Don't be afraid, Woody. You're among friends. You've been invited to this place in this time on this day at this hour for a reason. Just as you were once summoned to help another, now it is your turn to be guided. I've been chosen for the task, as you had been chosen in the past.'

As I intuited her words, I knew she was talking about Violetta. Indeed, Trumpet Man had told me that I had been 'chosen' by unseen forces to help Violetta find her way to her deceased parents some 25 years ago. Suddenly, the words emanating from Emma Jane's mouth matched the movement of her lips, and I knew we were back in real time, where she was just concluding her introduction of the next song. Her words froze me in my seat. I couldn't know it yet, but I would soon realize that the song she had chosen would echo the very words spoken to me by Armstrong only a few days ago.

# Chapter Seventeen

"This song is for you, Woody," Emma Jane announced, concluding her introduction.

With that, the stage lights dimmed and the three of them hunkered down into a deliciously sexy, instrumental version of a song that somehow sounded familiar to me, although I couldn't draw its title to mind. The audience was definitely groovin' on this one! Bodies rocked from side to side in their seats, and eyes closed in appreciation. For this song, Caden Michael was sitting at his trap set, on a riser high above his percussion lair at center stage, layin' down a slick Swing beat accentuated by metal brushes rather than wooden sticks. Chelsea Miranda traded her guitar for an electric bass and masterfully held her beautifully crafted lines behind the beat. Emma Jane joined in on electric piano filling in the harmonic structure. I suddenly recognized the song to be an old Cole Porter standard, "It's All Right With Me." Emma Jane leaned into the microphone on its stand at the piano and looked out into the hall, her eyes finding me easily and purposefully. When she began to sing, time stood still.

*"It's the wrong time, and the wrong place..."*

All the while, she stared directly into my eyes, as if to accentuate the words she was singing solely for me.

My eyes welled up with salty tears. When their Papa had so startled me 25 years ago, I became terrified, unable to comprehend what was happening. But this time, I felt not a trace of fear. Rather, a smile took over my face, and the tears that rolled down my cheeks were tears of joy, not tears of fear. For I knew exactly what was happening this time, and I knew that *they* knew the twists of fate that I had endured, and it was their calling, indeed their mission, to guide me home, wherever and whenever that might be. If anyone or anything could reunite me with Violetta, I knew they could...and would. Indescribable warmth overtook my soul, and I felt Trumpet Man's presence behind all this. My mind was flooded with cascading images and remembrances of The Performer, Violetta, Mario and Maria, indeed all the people I had encountered on my travels 25 years earlier. I closed my eyes and bowed my head in thanks, ready to continue my predestined journey.

The remainder of the show passed like a flash. Before I knew it, the audience had filed out of the hall after two or three demanded encores, leaving me sitting alone in the middle of the auditorium. The stage lights now dim and the house lights up full, the three of them bounded off the stage, holding hands, bouncing up the aisle towards me. No longer weak in the knees, I stood.

"What a terrific show..." I started to gush.

Before I could get another word out, Emma Jane threw herself at me, flinging her arms around me with a loving hug.

"Woody...I can't begin to tell you how glad I am you've found us," she whispered into my ear.

I stepped back from her embrace, looking directly into her beautiful eyes, before I answered.

"I can't tell you how glad I am I've found you, either, Emma Jane! The last time I saw you, you were…"

"I know, I know," she laughed. "I was only this big!" she said, leveling her right hand only a foot above the floor.

The other two musicians stood at her side, a bit uncomfortable at not having been properly introduced as yet. Chelsea Miranda actually nudged Emma Jane as if to cue her to proceed according to plan.

Suddenly, I knew who I was supposed to have met that Sunday afternoon 25 years ago, the day after my doomed performance with Violetta at the Ellicott Club. I recalled my phone conversation with Cassie, Trumpet Man's wife, as she told me about two people I needed to meet when I was to have visited her and the *Rochester* Emma Jane that next day.

"You must be Jessica's youngest," I smiled to the blushing young man in front of me, "for your eyes are your sister's eyes, without question!"

To my surprise but delight, Caden Michael put his arms around me and hugged me gently before answering, a nervous giggle audible.

"I'm so glad to finally meet you, Woody…even it *is* 25 years late!"

"And *you*," I offered, looking at Chelsea Miranda, "must be Jennifer's child."

Chelsea Miranda nodded vigorously, never ceasing to smile, and unabashedly hugged me so as not to be left out of this little love fest.

"Are you guys hungry?" I asked, knowing in advance what their answer would be.

"We could eat a horse!" they chimed in unison.

"Well, what are waiting for? I know a great little restaurant nearby. They've got…" I began to say only to be interrupted by Emma Jane.

"…the best grilled cheese sandwiches around!" she finished.

The four of us left the theater arm in arm, with no need of any additional spoken words.

# Chapter Eighteen

*Thomas*

After my shift at the Williamsport Best Western Hotel, I drove home, eager for a good night's sleep. No sooner did I open my garage door and drive my car in than something began to tug at the edges of my thoughts. I couldn't quite put my finger on it, but I knew that it would come to me if I stopped thinking about it. So I brewed a pot of tea, turned on the all-night Jazz show I listened to on public radio every night, and plopped down in my easy chair in the living room with my newspaper, fulfilling my daily ritual of catching up on the world news. I purposely avoided thinking about whatever was trying to pry its way into my conscious thoughts, confident that by ignoring it I would in fact allow it to come forward in full bloom.

As usually happens, about fifteen minutes into reading the paper my eyelids started feeling heavy, closing as an invitation to sleep. On the radio in the background, I could faintly hear an old arrangement of tenor saxophonist Coleman Hawkins and singer Sarah Vaughn performing "Body and Soul," Sarah providing the luscious body to Coleman's emotive soul. All at once, my eyes flew open, and my mind returned to full awareness. What was bothering me under all those layers of my consciousness was the visit earlier in the evening from another saxophonist, Woody Reed. Out of the blue after 25 years, he had come into the restaurant, as if no more than a week or two had passed since I last saw him. He asked about Violetta, the singer he had performed with for the first time at the hotel all those years ago. I told him that I hadn't heard another word about Violetta after reading in the paper that she had been badly burned in the fire that had destroyed a Rochester club, the name of which escaped me at the moment. He looked like his world was about to fall apart at the seams when I told him that. But sitting here now, I suddenly remembered that Violetta *had* come into the restaurant maybe three or four months *after* her gig at the hotel, asking about Woody! In fact, I remember she came in with a friend, who told me she was a waitress in Rochester. We talked about that for at least ten minutes, which is surely how I came to remember the visit. Truth be told, I was somewhat taken with her friend, but neither the time nor place seemed appropriate to initiate the kind of relationship I might have wanted back then.

I spent the next half-hour feeling totally guilty that I hadn't remembered this visit when Woody had asked me earlier in the evening. I finally convinced myself I shouldn't beat myself up too badly. It was, after all, 25 years ago, so I could be forgiven a momentary lapse of memory. I wracked my brain, trying to remember if Woody had told me where he was headed this night. The more I thought about it, the more I was sure that he never did tell me. I suspected this new information might help his search, if not his frame of mind. But for the life of me, I had no idea how to contact him. If only I had thought to ask for his address or phone number...

# Chapter Nineteen

*Violetta*

After my all-night conversation with Briggett, I slept late the next morning, emotional exhaustion draining my energy as surely as physical fatigue must have claimed hers. I woke up around noon to the sound of a light rain tinkling against the bedroom window, despite the coldness of winter that had until now trapped us in its icy grip. I lay there in bed for another ten minutes, mesmerized by the sounds of the house. Finally getting out of bed before dozing off again, I shuffled into the kitchen to find a note that Briggett had left on the table.

> *V,*
> *I'm off to work. Help yourself to whatever you need. Here's a spare house key,*
> *in case you go out. I'll be home by about 11:00 tonight.*
> *See you then…we'll talk some more. In fact, I have an idea!*
> *Later…*
> *Brig*

I found the coffeepot right away and brewed some Cinnamon Hazelnut, which was in its bag in the refrigerator door, properly labeled. This was Woody's favorite coffee, and that recollection stabbed at my heartstrings like a dagger. After downing a couple of cups, I made myself some scrambled eggs and wheat toast, content to wile away the day absorbed in mundane tasks. Frankly, I welcomed the break from my troubled and obsessive thoughts about finding Woody. I knew it would do me good to spend a mindless day in this warm, quiet house, without so much as a thought about the weather or anything else. So that's exactly what I did. After a long hot bath, I spent the rest of the day dressed only in the bathrobe Briggett had left hanging near the tub for me, reading yesterday's paper, and snacking on leftovers. I looked forward to Briggett coming home later in the evening and sharing her idea with me. Although I'd just met her, I felt that I'd found a true friend, indeed a life-long friend, someone who would never think to say or do anything to hurt me.

Around ten o'clock that evening, I decided to prepare a dinner of pasta marinara for the two of us, figuring Briggett would be exhausted from her day waiting tables. Although no one ever would have called me a good cook, I managed to do an adequate job of playing chef, and by eleven I had the table set awaiting her return. Sure enough, like clockwork, I heard her key in the lock minutes later. She strolled in looking none the worse for wear.

"What's *this*?" she asked, gesturing to the table, obviously surprised at what she was seeing and smelling there.

"Pasta Marinara," I answered proudly.

"I can see that, V, but you really didn't have to go to all the trouble!"

"Oh, it was no trouble, Brig. Besides, it's the least I could do. I don't know many people who would offer their house to a stranger like you've done. Consider this my small way of saying *thanks for being a friend.*"

"I must admit, I'm pretty hungry," she said, turning away to prevent me from seeing her blush. She put her raincoat onto its hanger and hung it in the closet near the front door.

She took a couple of candles down from the cupboard, lit them, and placed them on the table. We enjoyed a comfortable dinner, talking about her day at the Frog Pond. When it was apparent that our conversation was running out of steam, she got up from her chair and began to clear the dishes from the table, all the while looking at me to gauge if she thought I was ready to proceed to more serious matters. I helped her, she rinsing and me loading the dishwasher. When we finished, we ambled into the living room to relax. She sat down on an overstuffed pillow on the dark wooden floor, her back against the wall. I sat cross-legged across the small room, elbows resting on my knees, already beginning to wonder about the idea she had earlier hinted at.

"I have an idea, V," she said abruptly.

I didn't answer, instead waiting for her to continue.

"If you're ever going to find out what happened to Woody, we have to look for him on the assumption he can't look for you," she said with conviction.

"I thought that's what I *was* doing when I searched *you* out," I answered with nowhere near the same level of assurance.

"Okay, finding me was a good start, V. But we've got to go back and trace your steps, visit all the places you were together. Sooner or later, we're bound to find something. Listen…tomorrow's my day off. I think we should get an early start and visit the Ellicott Club."

"But the place burned down, Brig. I don't see how…" I stammered, feeling my eyes starting to sting from holding back the tears.

"...I know, I know, but it can't hurt. You never know what we might find there. And if that doesn't turn up anything, we'll take another step back in time. It's the only way, V. The worst that can happen is we'll waste a day looking. What do you say?"

Of course, she was right. I agreed to her plan, despite my fear at what we might actually find in the process. But I had no better idea.

We retreated to our separate rooms, intent on being well rested for our morning stakeout at the Ellicott Club, or what was left of it.

# Chapter Twenty

*Thomas*

Having recalled Violetta asking about Woody 25 years ago, I had to do *something* or I would never sleep tonight! I logged onto the Internet and did a search for *Woody Reed, saxophonist, Rochester, NY.* Sure enough, I found a number of links which listed his discography, groups he had performed with, and accolades from various reviewers. To my disappointment, there was no listing showing address or phone number. I was about to give up and log off when my eye barely caught a link to a bulletin board message that had been sent out into cyberland by Woody only a few days ago.

*Violetta: if you see this message, please contact me.*
*Woody*

I clicked on *Reply* and typed a message.

*Woody,*

*After you left the restaurant this evening, I suddenly remembered that Violetta had indeed visited the hotel once about 25 years ago, looking for you! I'm afraid it just slipped my mind after all that time.*

*In fact, she came in with a friend, a waitress she knew in Rochester. (I think her name was Briggett.) I sincerely hope this helps you.*
  *All the best to you, my friend...*
  *Thomas*

I clicked *Send Message,* secure in the knowledge that perhaps I'd done my small part in helping Woody solve his mystery. With that, I collapsed into bed and slept the night away, unfettered by any lingering negative thoughts.

# Chapter Twenty-One

*Woody*

Within minutes of leaving the Kimball Theatre in separate cars, our little caravan arrived at the restaurant I remembered from my visits here with The Performer 25 years ago. To my surprise, the place hadn't changed a bit. And it was still empty of customers at this hour, which made me wonder how they managed to pay their bills! Regardless, we had our choice of tables, selecting one fronting a window looking out onto Richmond Road. There was a light rain falling outside, and I found the pitter-patter on the window quite relaxing. A young waiter approached our table, depositing four menus for our review, unable to take his eyes off Emma Jane or Chelsea Miranda. Caden Michael noticed and giggled softly to himself.

"May I bring you a drink while you look at the menu?" he asked.

The four of us answered at the same instant.

"I'll have your house ginger ale, please," we chimed in unrehearsed unison.

The waiter didn't know what to make of this turn of events, merely shaking his head and turning to return to the bar for our drinks. We four, on the other hand, laughed uproariously, looking at each other in mild disbelief.

"Our Papa wore that line out years ago!" laughed Emma Jane.

"You can say that again!" Chelsea Miranda agreed.

"Hee, hee," chuckled Caden Michael.

"If I remember correctly," I interrupted, "this place boasted the best grilled cheese sandwiches in town. Some things never change, I guess."

The waiter returned with our four ginger ales. Before he could even ask, we all ordered a grilled cheese sandwich, which further caught him off guard. He departed looking like he couldn't wait to get away from the four strange people at his table, they being we four! Once the giggling stopped, I knew I had to ask the question. I suspected I already knew the answer, but I had to ask.

"And what of your Papa?" I struggled.

Their eyes answered my question better than words could. It was Emma Jane who spoke first.

"Woody...he's still with us," she said, with her hand over her heart.

"Actually, we visit him often," added Chelsea Miranda, her eyes fixed on Emma Jane's hand.

"Yeah," said Caden Michael, "and last time we were with him he told us we needed to take care of you. He said you'd understand when we told you it was time to get back on the horse...said he had told you that once before, so you were sure to realize what he meant by that. *Do* you, Woody?"

"Yes, I do," I answered deliberately and without hesitation.

"Then it's settled," Emma resolved. "Tomorrow night, you sit in with us Woody, at the theater. Que sera, sera."

"It sounds so simple, doesn't it?" I asked.

"It's the only way, Woody," Emma concluded.

The waiter returned to our table with four identical grilled cheese platters. It seemed that each enjoyed his or her meal more than the other. We spent the rest of the evening talking about their Papa. I told them all about my first visit to Williamsburg and the Kimball Theatre some 25 years ago, yet but a week in my time frame. But they already knew all about my first meeting with their Papa, not to mention my performances with Violetta.

"Meet us at the back stage entrance to the theater tomorrow night at 7:30, Woody," Emma Jane concluded. "I'm sure you remember where it is."

"Oh, I remember, all right," I answered with a smile and a nod of the head.

With that, the four of us stood and departed the restaurant together, arms around shoulders in a line not unlike a chorus of dancers on stage. I began to feel that my journey had a purpose, one that might actually return me to the right time and place.

# Chapter Twenty-Two

*Briggett*

Exhausted as I was after a long day at the Frog Pond, I slept like a log, waking up before my alarm clock had a chance to violate the next morning's solitude. I took a quick shower and dressed in record time, thinking I would fix breakfast for the two of us. To my surprise, Violetta was already in the kitchen putting the finishing touches on homemade pancakes. I chuckled out loud, thinking I could easily get used to having someone cook my meals for me. Dinner last night, and now breakfast…this was just too much to ask for!

It was still dark outside, and a steady snow was falling. With pancakes stuck to our ribs and coffee adding the required caffeine kick, we threw our coats and boots on, eager to get on the road to begin our search for any clues to Woody's whereabouts. By 7:30, we were on our way to the downtown corner where the Ellicott Club had once stood. As we drove up, I can't say we were surprised to see an empty lot. After all, the building had burned to the ground. But the total completeness of the cleanup did catch us a bit off guard. It looked like nothing had ever stood here before. Grass and shrubs had been planted, already managing to stick up through the steadily accumulating snow. We just sat there in the car, hesitant to look at each other, listening to the defroster motor breaking the discomfort of our dead silence. As if on cue, we both opened our car doors at the same time, getting out to walk the site, wondering if some magical intuition would fall upon us.

It was so quiet outside you could actually hear the heavy, wet snow blanketing the ground in a self-protective barrier to our prying eyes. No sooner did we walk across the site than our footprints were already covered over by fresh snow. It was easy to imagine that no one had ever been here before, to say nothing of a building having stood here. Don't ask me why, but I actually thought about all the times I'd visited Niagara Falls, wondering what it must have looked like to the first Indian ever to approach the hypnotic waters of the raging Niagara River as it sought the solace of the rocks so far below. I never wondered why some people jumped, unable to step away from the edge. It was that strong a pull on the human psyche.

I can't say that Violetta looked disappointed. In truth, I'm sure she expected to find nothing of value here. I think I was more dejected than she was, perhaps because I had every expectation of finding something…anything…that would lead us to Woody. It was only then that I realized I may have even felt at least a touch of jealousy over Violetta's relationship with Woody, one that I would have welcomed and indeed had invited teasingly, perhaps too modestly to achieve my goal. More to break the silence than anything else, I spoke first.

"Well, V…what now?" I asked.

"Are you in the mood for a little drive," she finally answered after several long moments of pondering the situation.

"Absolutely," I agreed. "Where to?"

"Williamsport PA…" she chimed…"the hotel where Woody and I met and performed for the first time together."

"Let's do it," I urged.

In this weather, the drive would be a long and arduous one, especially once we reached the mountains of northern Pennsylvania. So we drove back to my place and packed a small suitcase for each of us, just in case we would need to stay over the night, which I suspected we would. In good weather, we would have made it to Williamsport before noon. But today would be different, I knew, and we both seemed to steel ourselves for the drive that awaited us. I figured we'd be lucky to make it there by dinnertime. But that didn't stop us.

# Chapter Twenty-Three

*Violetta*

Briggett took the first driving shift. We drove her car because it had all-wheel drive, making it the obvious choice over my bus. The bad news was that the snow continued to fall heavily. The good news was that there was not a hint of wind, so the wet snow didn't blow or drift, making the driving not at all tiresome, despite having to proceed well below any posted speed limits. I suspect we had both learned long ago from living in this climate that when it came to traveling in wintertime, the tortoise invariably arrived at his destination well before the hare.

As I suspected would be the case, the weather took a dramatic turn for the worse as soon as we approached the higher terrain of southern New York, appropriately known as The Southern Tier. The farther we drove up into the hills, the more difficult it became. What began as inches of snow in Rochester quickly became feet of snow here, and the earlier calm was replaced by gusty winds buffeting the car on all sides. We pressed on, knowing that conditions would probably change once we crested the hills and began our descent into the Pennsylvania valley. Despite the 55-mph speed limit, we never drove faster than 30-mph, preferring to maintain a steady and safe pace. We both shook our heads in disbelief at the number of SUV drivers who recklessly passed us, skidding and fishtailing in the unplowed left lane. Sure enough, we passed most of them mere minutes later, digging their vehicles out of roadside ditches. Didn't these people comprehend the value of patience?

By around noontime, we were through the hills and heading into the valley beyond. True to our suspicion, the sun was actually attempting to peek through the thick dark clouds. What had been heavy snowfall only minutes ago in the highlands of New York was a light dusting in the valleys of Pennsylvania. But we didn't kid ourselves. We both knew that as soon as we left the valley and continued on towards Williamsport, we would have to drive through yet another section of mountainous terrain where the weather would certainly take a turn for the worse again. We stopped for gas, refilled the windshield-washer with fluid, and decided to have lunch at a roadside diner. Despite the neon "Truckers Welcome" sign in the front window, there were no trucks parked in the lot, and only a few cars. The diner was an Art Deco prototype from the nineteen-fifties, so common in this part of the country.

We walked in the front door where another sign awaited us: "Please Seat Yourself." So, we did, preferring a vinyl-clad booth to rotating stools at the counter. Once unburdened of our coats, we sat down and looked over the menu. A heavy-set waitress who looked to be about fifty quickly approached our table, as if sensing that we had made a decision on what to order.

"What can I get you, sweetie," she asked Briggett.

"Ohhh...I think I'd like the open-faced turkey sandwich with mashed potatoes and gravy," Briggett mused somewhat comically, probably afraid of my reaction to her ordering such a large meal so early in the day.

"Make it two," I added quickly, smiling across the table in answer to Briggett's surprised expression. "Hey, we're on an adventure, right?" I offered in explanation, not that one was required or expected.

"That we are, V," she quipped. "That we are!"

Forty-five minutes later, we were both ready for a nap! The turkey sandwiches were simply wonderful, the mashed potatoes fresh and creamy, and the gravy thick and tasty. I'm sure we looked like we were ready to slump over the table in search of relief from our meals, which must have been the waitress's cue to hurry back over.

"Can I get you anything else, sweetie?" she asked, this time looking directly at me, not Briggett.

"How about a couple of pillows and blankets?" I joked, which brought out a chuckle from the three of us.

"What's for dessert?" Briggett interrupted.

I just looked at her from across the table in disbelief.

"You must be kidding!" I laughed out loud.

Without wasting a moment, the waitress rattled off a long list of desserts all made fresh on the premises. Briggett caught my attention with a hilarious wide-eyed look that seemed to say *'let's go for it.'* So we did.

"I'll have apple pie a la mode," I gushed, almost ashamed of myself.

"I'd like cherry cobbler a la mode," Briggett ventured.

"And two strong coffees," I added.

The waitress smiled broadly and headed to the pie case to begin preparations.

"Are we nuts or what?" I asked Briggett in mock anger.

"Nuts? Oh, V, we forgot to ask for nuts…"

The waitress must have heard us, for moments later our pies arrived, each with a dollop of real whipped cream topped with a sprinkle of nuts.

"This," marveled Briggett, "is heaven."

"Yup…you only live once, Brig," I chuckled.

As we sat there, enjoying each other's company as if life-long friends, I had the strangest sensation that I really knew absolutely nothing about her. Here she was, trying to help me put my life back in order, and I hadn't even bothered to ask her about her own life. Was that selfishness? Or, was it being so wrapped up in my own problems that I never even thought anyone else could have problems? Or, was there really a difference between the two?

"Brig," I began. "You know, it just occurred to me that I don't know a thing about you, other than you're the best friend I ever had, you're a friend of Woody, you're a wonderful waitress, and you're one of the kindest people I've ever met!"

I could see her blush mightily at my words, before being overcome with emotion in a way that surprised me.

"Don't get me going, V," she answered. "I'm really nobody special. I just like helping people. And there you were, someone who needed my help."

"But that's exactly what I mean, Brig. People who help other people have usually been helped by someone else, and they feel like they need to pay back the kindness by helping others."

She looked inward for a moment before answering, and when she spoke her words were slow and deliberate.

"I guess that's true in my case, too, V," she admitted. "I guess I feel that by helping you, I'm helping myself at the same time. I hope that doesn't sound too selfish."

"Selfish? Don't be ridiculous!" I admonished her.

She paused for a few moments before deciding it was okay to tell me more, which surely must have been an indication that she trusted me as much as I trusted her, despite the reality that we had known each other for such a short time.

"You see, V, my life really isn't all that different than yours," she continued. "And maybe that's why I was drawn to help you. Like you, I lost my parents, too. Yours died in a car accident. Mine died in a plane crash. Like you, I was young, maybe sixteen years old. And suddenly, I found myself totally alone in this world, an only child with no parents."

"Oh, Brig...I'm so sorry," I said across the table. "You don't have to tell me any more if you don't want to. I know exactly how you feel, believe me, I do."

At that moment, she took a deep breath and smiled at me.

"V, I've never spoken to anyone else about this. But talking to you, I feel like it's okay to let it out and get it off my chest. For some reason, it doesn't hurt right now, knowing that we share so much in our lives without ever knowing it before now. Like you, V, I had a guardian angel in my life, too."

"Who, Briggett?"

"Well," she mused, "I never really knew him. But the house I now live in? That was my parents' house. After they died, I just...well...kept living there, even as a sixteen year-old kid. I kept going to school, and just took care of myself. Nobody asked, and I never told anyone about living there alone. Then, maybe a month later, I received a registered letter from a lawyer, telling me that the mortgage on the house had been paid off in full, and I was the recipient of a trust fund which had just been set up in my name. Sure enough, about two weeks later the checks started coming, one every month, with enough money for me to live on...and a little left over."

125

"Brig...this is so much like my own story, it's uncanny. Didn't you ever want to know who this person was?" I pressed with genuine interest.

"Actually, V, I *did* want to know. In fact, I can admit to a certain morbid fascination about knowing. So, I visited the lawyer's office one day and proceeded to walk in and demand some answers. Imagine, a sixteen year-old kid making demands on an estate lawyer."

She paused again, as if trying to remember every detail before telling me more.

"Come on, Brig," I demanded. "You're killin' me here! What happened?"

"Luckily, this lawyer was a kind man, V. He just smiled at me, invited me to sit with him in his office, and asked his secretary to brew a pot of tea for us. Can you imagine? And there I sat, for two hours, drinking tea with this kindly old gentleman, as he told me all he could about my guardian."

"What do you mean, *'all he could'*, Brig?"

"Well, that's where it all got very interesting. It seems that my parents' life insurance policy was enough to pay off the mortgage on the house. But when I asked him where the monthly checks were coming from, he said he couldn't tell me any more than he already had."

"What does *that* mean, Brig? After all, it's your life you're talking about, right?"

Briggett looked right at me with the strangest look in her eyes.

"V...that's exactly what I said to the lawyer!" she explained. "Finally, he must have taken pity on me, because he offered to provide one piece of information if I promised never to act on it."

"Briggett, this is all getting very strange!" I gushed. "What did he tell you?"

"You ready for this, Violetta?"

"*Ready?* If you don't spill the beans right now I'm gonna toss this coffee at you!"

Briggett laughed. She was thoroughly enjoying this, I could tell. And it made me feel better inside that she trusted me enough to share her secret.

"Well…it seems that my mother had a brother. Growing up, she never really talked about him, other than to tell me that he was *an undesirable character.* Now, she wouldn't go into any detail, but the less she spoke of him the more I wanted to know. Then, out of the blue one day…I think I was about fifteen…she sat me down for one of those mother-daughter talks! I thought she was gonna tell me about the birds and the bees…of which I was already convinced I was an expert…but instead she started to tell me that if anything ever happened to her and Dad, her brother would take care of me. But she made me promise that I would never, ever, look for him, or attempt to communicate with him in any way."

"But…why, Brig?"

"I don't know, V," she pondered. "But I think there was something there that embarrassed her…that she was somehow ashamed of her own brother. No matter how hard I pressed her for answers, her lips were sealed. And that was that."

"*That's it?* That can't be the end of this story, Briggett!"

She smiled at me mischievously, purposely drawing out this tale of intrigue. If I thought my own life was different than the norm, I had become the victim of a rude awakening in the hearing of Briggett's life story!

"Yes, there's more, V! About a month later, I was in the car with my father, running some inconsequential errand for Mom. As casually as possible, I just asked him about Mom's brother…"

This story was getting hot! I couldn't control my excitement.

"What did he say, Brig?"

She laughed some more, almost unable to get the words out before finally calming down enough to speak. I didn't know if she was excited about what happened, or about my reaction to it, but I just kept looking at her with a look of expectation, virtually begging her with me eyes to tell me more.

"Get this, V," she answered. "My Dad very nonchalantly said *'Oh, you mean your uncle Leo?'* "

"You're kidding! Just like that?"

"Yup...just like that," she answered with a snap of her fingers. "Obviously, Dad had no idea that Mom and I had had a mother-daughter conversation the previous month. Or, if he *did* know, he never said anything about it. So I answered him *'yeah, Uncle Leo, Dad.'*"

"Aaaannnnnnd?"

"And Dad started laughing in a way I'd never heard him laugh before, right from his gut! Then he looked over at me in the seat next to him and said *'If you ever tell your Mom I told you this, I'll be knee-deep in kaka, Briggett! Can you keep our secret?'* I told him I could and would, so he chuckled again before answering *'Your Uncle Leo is a gangster, Briggett.'* "

"A gangster!" I howled. "Oh, my God, I can't believe this, Brig! Did you ever find out any more about him?"

"Not a thing," she answered with a look of disappointment. "Other than my Dad telling me that Uncle Leo's full name was Leonardo. My Mom's maiden name was Divencenzo, so that meant that I had a gangster uncle named Leonardo Divencenzo. Kind of sounds like a gangster's name, doesn't it?"

"I'll say it does...straight out of a TV script. And you never met him, or heard any more about him?"

"Nope, that was it. Oh, a couple of times I thought about how exciting it would be to try to find him, but I was a kid. I didn't know where to start. I didn't know if he lived in the same city...or country, for that matter!"

"So all this time, you just kept getting checks from a trust fund your Uncle Leo had obviously set up for you, and you never wanted to find out more?"

"Oh, I wanted to, V. But the lawyer told me I was never allowed to know where the money came from. And then, about three or four months ago, the checks stopped coming, just like they had started years earlier."

"You're kidding!" I said in disbelief. "Did you call the lawyer and ask him why?"

"As a matter of fact, I did."

"What did he say, Brig?"

"He invited me over for tea the next day. As we sat there, drinking and talking, he told me how sorry he was to have to be the one to inform me of the tragic news that my uncle had died. I said *'You mean my Uncle Leo?'* He just looked at me with the strangest look, wondering how I had known my uncle's name. And then he explained very politely that he was prohibited from telling me any more about my Uncle Leo, other than the fact that his will was tied up in court and wouldn't be unsealed for several years. He promised to keep me informed of the progress, but warned me *'not to inquire into this matter again.'* "

At that, Briggett threw up her hands in a gesture of surrender. Looking at her now reminded of the time I told Woody my own strange story of woe. I remembered that it felt like a giant boulder being lifted from my shoulders. I'm sure that's how Briggett felt at this moment. I felt the same sense of relief for her that I had felt for myself. But there was something else I was feeling. As we prepared to leave the diner, I couldn't shake the sensation that there was some important piece missing from this puzzle. The more I tried to put my finger on it, the more it drifted from my conscious thoughts.

# Chapter Twenty-Four

Duly fortified by the strong coffee, we were back on the road by 1:45, feeling none the worse for wear. We decided I would drive the next leg, since I was more familiar with this route, one that I had traveled many times before in between gigs. The weather fulfilled its promise of worse to come as we traveled the winding roads into the mountainous terrain surrounding Williamsport. Before we had even a moment to question our decision to continue, we found ourselves smack dab in the middle of what could only be described as a major blizzard. The snow was piling up relentlessly. The wind gusted viciously, making it virtually impossible to see more than a foot in front of the car. We slowed to a crawl. Under normal conditions, I always tried to avoid driving behind a truck on mountain roads. I dreaded the thought of not being able to see *through* the truck. I wanted to know what was ahead of it at all times, thinking this knowledge would somehow make me a better driver. But I absolutely hated the constant slowdown required when the truck lost its momentum as it struggled to climb each and every hill. That drove me crazy! But in this weather, I was actually comforted to be behind a semi, its tail lights a veritable beacon of hope in the storm. Never mind that the trucker might be as blind as we were! One naturally assumed a professional over-the-road driver was much more accustomed to arriving safely at his destination, despite the weather. Did you ever notice that it's easier to see clearly what's going on *behind* you when you're driving in a storm? As difficult as it was to see in front of us, we could easily see that a caravan of perhaps a dozen cars had formed behind us, each relying on the one in front of it to lead the way, and all counting on the assumed skills of the trucker.

We turned on the radio to ease the tension of driving. But the terrain dictated that no station signal could be maintained for more than a few minutes, and the constant drift of the signal and static proved more irritating than the silence. Before long, I glanced over at Briggett in the front seat next to me. Her eyes closed, shoulders slumping, and head leaning against the passenger window, she was sound asleep. In that moment, I suddenly realized how strange life is. I felt like I had known Briggett my whole life. In truth, we had just met. As different as we may have been in our upbringing, our outlook on worldly matters, or anything else, none of that could change the fact that we had established an immediate connection. Certainly, there was no doubt that the connection was Woody. More important, Briggett and I genuinely liked each other. I found myself wondering if we would remain friends for life or whether she would join that list of acquaintances who are a meaningful part of your life today, but gone and forgotten tomorrow.

As I continued to drive while she slept so peacefully, I couldn't shake that strange feeling that I was overlooking something. Ever since Briggett had told me about her Uncle Leo, something had started to flicker under the surface of my conscious thoughts. As so often happens when you try so hard to figure out what's bothering you, the more you press, the less able you are to come up with a satisfactory answer. So I did what

I always did when confronted in this way. I just put it out of my mind, secure in the knowledge that as soon as I stopped thinking about it, the answer would naturally present itself. Such thoughts must have occupied my mind for more time than I could have imagined, because before I knew it I was approaching the bridge over the river into Williamsport. I glanced at the dashboard clock to see that it was nearly 5 o'clock, which meant that I had completely lost track of the last two hours. The truck slowed to 5 mph on the bridge, mindful of icy patches, and his caravan followed suit. Of course, I assumed the driver was a *he,* but it wouldn't have surprised me it he were a *she!* I put on my right blinker to indicate I would be leaving the expressway at the first exit. The truck's rear lights blinked rapidly, as if to say *I got you this far, now be careful the rest of the way.* I was stunned how thankful this little gesture made me feel, reminding me once again that we're not all that different from each other. As I exited, the rest of the caravan moved forward behind the truck so as not to leave a broken link in the chain. I actually waved as they passed.

I found my way to the hotel parking lot, thankful that it was already in the process of being plowed out, despite the continuing snowfall. Perhaps sensing the change in driving conditions since I had left the expressway, Briggett awoke to the realization that we had safely arrived at our destination.

"We're there?" she asked groggily.

"And in one piece," I joked, relieved to be free of the pressures of driving through the blizzard.

"How long have I been sleeping, V?"

"Oh, I don't know…a couple of hours, maybe," I answered.

"I'm sorry, V…I just couldn't keep my eyes open for another second," Briggett apologized.

"Don't be silly, Brig! After all, *you're* the one who worked late last night, remember?"

She smiled in recognition of my appreciation for her efforts, not to mention her companionship. I parked her car right in the front lot, which had already been cleared, leaving only a short walk to the hotel entrance. We were traveling light, each with only a small overnight bag, so we were in the lobby registering for a room within a minute. The desk clerk was one I didn't recognize from previous visits here. She looked up from her computer as Briggett ventured to a coffee bar to fill two plastic cups.

"Good evening," she offered politely. "May I help you?"

"Yes, please," I answered. "I'd like a non-smoking room for the night."

"Certainly!" she said.

Within minutes, coffee cups in hand, Briggett and I rode the elevator up to the seventh floor, which was reserved for non-smoking guests. As I opened the door, I was irritated by the fact that I had forgotten to ask for a room with two double beds in favor of this room with a king size bed. But I was immediately struck by the coincidence that this was the very same room Woody had brought me to that night after our first journey to The Zone together. I stood there, in the open doorway, gazing around the room as if afraid to enter.

"What's the matter, V?" Briggett asked. "You look like you've seen a ghost."

"Brig, by some strange coincidence, this is the very same room that Woody and I shared after our first performance together," I answered haltingly.

Briggett's jaw dropped as she continued watching me look around the room. All at once, she took control of the situation, grabbing my bag from my hand and literally pushing me forward into the room so she could close the door behind us.

"There are no coincidences in this life, V," she said with conviction, which startled me out of my dizziness. "Everything happens for a reason, even if we can never know the reason. This is a *sign*, V! And a *good* sign, at that! I can feel it in my bones. We're on the right track. Somewhere, someone is leading you to Woody."

I could think of nothing more appropriate for the moment than to throw my arms around Briggett, which is exactly what I did. Standing there, I realized that she was patting my back, like a mother would to comfort her fearful child.

"You go ahead and shower, V," Briggett insisted. "I'll unpack our stuff and wait 'til you're done."

"You sure, Brig? I don't mind waiting…"

"…no argument, young lady!" she interrupted.

I smiled and headed into the bathroom. Far be it from me to disobey an order so forcefully given!

# Chapter Twenty-Five

*Woody*

After we left the restaurant, Emma, Caden and Chelsea got into their own cars and departed. As I stood there, car keys in hand, I suddenly realized I hadn't even bothered to check into a motel upon arriving in Williamsburg this morning! On a whim, I turned right from the restaurant and within a few blocks I found the same little bungalow style motel where I'd stayed on my first visit here 25 years ago. The name of the place had changed, and the bungalows had been upgraded to a more modern appearance, but I felt a certain comfort in finding the place intact after all these years had passed. Although it wasn't late by cosmopolitan living standards, I reminded myself that this town pretty much rolled up its sidewalks by 9 o'clock in the evening. As I entered the motel office, I actually chuckled at the recollection of waking the desk clerk the first time I had stayed here. Here I was, doing it again 25 years later, although not to the same person, for these were new owners. I asked for the same bungalow I had previously enjoyed, and they accommodated my wish without question, perhaps used to the same request from countless tourists for reasons most of us would never comprehend or understand.

I parked my car in the designated spot and entered my bungalow. When I flicked on the light, the room appeared to have been remodeled quite recently. Much to my surprise, there was a small sign on the bureau indicating that Internet access was available 24/7/365, at no additional charge. Before even bothering to unpack my clothes, I grabbed my laptop from the outer zipper compartment of my suitcase and plugged into the modular phone outlet on the wall, labeled "Internet Access." I was eager to log on for any messages I might have received since leaving Rochester. After logging on with my password, the welcome screen came up, indicating one message in my Inbox. I clicked on it, and the moment the message came up on the screen, I felt my heart in my throat, beating uncontrollably. There, before my eyes, was a message from Thomas, the waiter at the Williamsport hotel, telling me that he had remembered Violetta coming back to look for me, after all, some 25 years ago. I choked back the tears, realizing that my search suddenly had new meaning, for Violetta had indeed been looking for me, even as I now searched for her a quarter of a century later. As I read over Thomas's message several times, I couldn't help but wonder about his mention of Briggett as the waitress who had come with Violetta to the hotel that day some 25 years ago. Was it possible that Violetta and Briggett had somehow come in contact with each other and decided to search for me together? The more I thought about it, the more I decided that the two of them were probably very much alike in ways that a man might not fully comprehend. If they were together, I had to admit that I felt a surge of warmth thinking that at least they had the benefit of each other's friendship, something I could only cherish at this moment.

I clicked on *Reply* and sent off a quick response to thank Thomas for his email:

*Thomas: I can't thank you enough for your message. Believe it or not, I think I may soon find Violetta, for I'm hot on the trail and hope to be reunited with her within the next days. I look forward to seeing you again one day…25 years ago! I'll explain it all then, Thomas. So keep the pasta marinara warm.*

*Your friend, Woody Reed*

# Chapter Twenty-Six

*Briggett*

Violetta and I relaxed in our room for a couple of hours, unwinding after a long hard day behind the wheel. At around 7:30 we rode the elevator down to the lobby and strolled into the restaurant to grab a light dinner before retiring for the night. Violetta was surprised that she didn't recognize anyone, including the hostess, despite the fact that she had performed here so often, most recently only several months ago. Regardless, we were seated at a table-for-two quite near the stage, although there was no performer scheduled this evening. Once again, Violetta's expression when we sat down set the tone for the conversation to follow.

"Brig, I know you're going to think I'm making this up, but this is the same table Woody sat at that first night when he came here and heard me perform!" she whispered despite the lack of anyone sitting near us.

I just looked around to get a feel for the room, trying to visualize the scene Violetta was describing to me in hushed tones. It was almost as if I had been here that night, it was that real in my own mind's eye.

"Like I said, V, there are no coincidences in life. Everything happens for a reason, even if we may never know the reason.

But it's another sign that we're on the right track, of that I have no doubt," I comforted her.

Moments later, the hostess walked back over to our table.

"I'm sorry, ladies, I'm afraid I forgot to ask if either of you would care for a drink before you order dinner," she explained with an embarrassed look on her face.

Violetta answered for the two of us.

"We'll both have your house ginger ale, please."

The hostess smiled at the humor and said, "Two house ginger ales, coming right up! Thomas will be your server this evening, and he'll return shortly with your drinks and menus."

Violetta's jaw hit the floor.

"What is it, V?" I asked.

"Brig," she answered catching her breath, "Thomas was here that night! He waited on Woody, and Thomas and I often spoke to each other on the many evenings I performed here. If anybody remembers Woody, it'll be Thomas!"

No sooner did Violetta finish her sentence than Thomas approached our table. Interestingly enough, he looked at me first, and I could have sworn he was about to flirt with me! But all at once he looked over to Violetta, and suddenly there were *two* jaws on the floor! This was all getting *interestinger and interestinger by the minute*, as they say.

"Violetta..." he stuttered.

"Thomas, I..." she stammered.

After a full 30-seconds of looking at each other in astonishment, I decided we'd be here all night unless *someone* said *something*, and it sure didn't look like either of them was capable of uttering a word.

"Thomas, my name is Briggett. I'm Violetta's best friend. Let's cut right to the chase. Have you seen Woody Reed?" I blurted out.

The question, put so bluntly, obviously had the intended effect. Thomas looked like he might fall over, so he rescued himself by pulling up an empty chair and sitting at our table. His face had turned white as ash, and his hands were shaking from the shock of the moment.

"Violetta," he began deliberately, "I'm afraid I haven't seen Woody since the last time you two performed here, what...three, maybe four months ago? The last I heard, you had a serious accident up in Rochester at some club, and you were severely injured. We didn't know what to think. What happened, anyway? And more important, are you okay?"

Violetta had a hard time hiding the look of disappointment. She tried to answer Thomas, but the words just couldn't escape her mouth, whereupon I again came to the rescue without need of invitation.

"Actually, Violetta is doing remarkably well, as you can see for yourself, Thomas," I clipped. "But she *must* find Woody. That's why we're here. Any help you can offer will be greatly appreciated."

Thomas turned his head to look right at me, and I saw great tenderness in those beautiful sad eyes of his.

"What did you say your name was?" he asked.

"Briggett," I answered.

"Briggett. That's a pretty name...for a lovely woman. Let me guess...you're a waitress, right?"

"How did you know that?" I wondered aloud.

"Oh, I don't know, it's just something about your manner of speaking. You know, no nonsense, get right to the point," he joked with a warm smile.

"So it's that obvious, huh?"

"I'm afraid so, Briggett. But to answer your question, I only met Woody that one time, the night he came in here for dinner and heard Violetta perform. Let's just say it was pretty apparent to all watching that he was immediately taken with her talent…not to mention beauty. The next thing we all knew, he was sitting in with her for the final set of the evening, and they brought this old room to life. I'll never forget it…greatest show I ever heard. But that was the last time I saw Woody, and indeed the last time I saw Violetta, too. I truly wish I could be more helpful, but I'm afraid the story ends as simply as it began."

Violetta reached out and took Thomas's hand in hers.

"Thanks, Thomas. To answer your question, I'm doing much better now. Let's just say I've been laid up for the past few months recuperating. But finding Woody is now the focus of my life. So, if…you know…"

Thomas looked back to Violetta and assured her.

"Of course, Violetta…if I see him, I'll tell him you were here looking for him. But…if you don't mind me asking, where does Briggett fit into this puzzle?"

"Oh, let's just say Briggett and I are old friends," Violetta answered.

"Man, I better become a musician! Two beautiful ladies looking for me? I should be so lucky!" Thomas laughed.

"Thanks, Thomas," Violetta answered in a whisper. "You'll be a great catch for some lucky lady soon, I'm sure."

With that, Thomas got up, replaced the chair at the empty table from which he had taken it, favored me with another almost-flirtatious look, and turned back for one final comment.

"Let me guess," he said with one raised eyebrow. "Two plates of pasta marinara with grilled vegetables, right?"

"The man is a born waiter," I joked to Violetta, thinking that if time allowed, Thomas and I might actually enjoy each other's company. I filed that away for later thought and action.

# Chapter Twenty-Seven

*Thomas*

Before going into work at the hotel the next afternoon, I logged on to retrieve my email messages. There was only one, and it was from Woody Reed:

*Thomas: I can't thank you enough for your message. Believe it or not, I think I may soon find Violetta, for I'm hot on the trail and hope to be reunited with her within the next days. I look forward to seeing you again one day...25 years ago! I'll explain it all then, Thomas. So keep the pasta marinara warm.*
*Your friend,*
*Woody Reed*

I had never received such a strange message before! *'I look forward to seeing you again? 25 years ago?'* What was *that* supposed to mean? Or, was it just a simple typo? I scratched my head, logged off the computer, and ventured out to another day of waiting tables. Life was just too strange these days for me to comprehend, I'm afraid.

# Chapter Twenty-Eight

*Violetta*

Briggett and I got an early wake-up call the next morning, leaving Williamsport by 7:00 a.m. We didn't even eat breakfast, preferring a head start on the day's destination, Williamsburg. The early morning weather was beautiful, with a gorgeous sunrise penetrating a cloudless sky as we pulled out of the hotel parking lot. The streets had been plowed during the night, and people were out and about on their way to work. We figured to get in a few hours of uninterrupted driving before stopping for breakfast somewhere near the Pennsylvania-Maryland border.

We had plenty to talk about, that's for sure! I don't know why I should have been surprised, but Briggett seemed quite taken with Thomas. Although the more I thought about it, the more I realized they probably would make a perfect couple, should they ever pursue the opportunity to get to know each other under more normal circumstances. Then again, *abnormal* circumstances often seemed to generate the best excuses for lasting relationships, providing a *reason* for communicating about important life issues rather than the usual mundane activities. After all, you sure couldn't pretend that the relationship I had with Woody had been mundane, short though it had been under the abnormal circumstances that I was still trying to figure out.

Brig and I were convinced that running into Thomas last night was a sign that we were on the right track to locating Woody, giving us hope of finding more clues in Williamsburg later this day. It was my intention to visit the Kimball Theatre, where Woody had performed with the person he so fondly referred to only as *The Performer* in the days before meeting me in Williamsport on his way back home to Rochester. Although I had never before visited Williamsburg, I had no doubt that we would have no trouble finding the theater. If we were lucky, we would even find The Performer still on the playbill. If not, we would have to search him out, which might be a bit more difficult without knowing his real name! Nothing abnormal about *that* expectation, right? Regardless, our moods remained upbeat as we drove, focusing only on the positive outcome we hoped to experience.

By mid-morning, hunger got the better of us, so we stopped at a pancake house in Amish country, parking Briggett's car next to several black-canopied, four-wheeled buggies still attached to their horses. We relaxed over muffins and coffee after devouring the main course of pancakes and scrambled eggs. Duly fortified, we were back on the road after a welcome 45-minute respite from driving. Since I had driven all morning, Brig drove for the next few hours. After another trade-off of driving duties, we found ourselves approaching Williamsburg in mid-afternoon. The sky was brilliant blue, the sun bright, with not a hint of a cloud in sight. Much to our delight, the mid-sixties temperature forced us to peel off our heavy winter coats in favor of the sweaters we both wore underneath. Indeed, it was warm enough to open the car windows halfway. We could easily have been fooled into believing it was a late-Spring day in Rochester. We followed the signs to the historic district and found a parking spot on one of the side streets. From there, it didn't take long to find the theater, located on Merchants Square in the heart of the retail shopping section of the world famous colonial area.

The theater was just as Woody had described it to me, an impressive and old-looking brick façade right on the square. I felt like I had been here before, if only in my imagination based on Woody's tale. We quickly walked up to the marquis that displayed a schedule of the month's movies and musical events, and there, staring us in the face, was a picture of The Performer!

'*A Tribute to American Music with the 21st Century Orchestra,*' read the marquee poster. We read further, and soon appreciated the comedic impact with the sub-headline, '*This ONE-MAN 21st Century Orchestra performs 20th Century standards by Errol Garner, Hoagy Carmichael, Duke Ellington, Cole Porter, George Gershwin, Billie Holiday, and more!*' A small crowd was lined up at the box office to purchase their tickets for tonight's show, so I figured if we hoped to get a seat, we'd better buy our tickets now!

Tickets in pocket, Briggett and I spent the next couple of hours walking down Duke of Gloucester Street, the main drag through the heart of Colonialand. Sure enough, it was just as Woody had described it, a thoroughly relaxing stroll through a few hundred years of American history, with no cars or modern inconveniences to get in the way. We decided to grab a bite to eat at Shields Tavern, the same place Woody had eaten before first seeing The Performer at the Kimball Theatre. Our waiter played the role of a young colonial gentleman…at least, I *think* it was a role…and we both enjoyed the tavern's special meal of grilled polenta with vegetables. At 7:30, we left the tavern with enough time to walk the mile or so back to the theater.

We were at the Kimball's front door by 7:45, along with a couple hundred other people. As we all entered, our tickets were taken by one of several ladies identifying themselves as theater volunteers. Through two sets of double doors, we entered the actual theater. I carefully picked out two seats right in the middle of the hall, hoping for the best acoustics, and craned my neck to see a large chandelier overhead. The seats were upholstered in plush velvet, the floor carpeted, the ceiling rounded and high, and the stage large and impressive, graced by the oversized burgundy colored curtains one would expect in a theater of this period. At center stage was a metal rack of electronic gear, on wheels, about three feet high. From the bottom snaked several long wires that were plugged into the stage floor. I surmised these must have been audio cables connected to the house sound system. I turned back in my seat and noticed above me, in the rear left of the hall, a small balcony, which must contain the house sound and light boards. I faced the stage once again, and noticed what appeared to be the screen of a laptop computer jutting out above the top of the rack. That, I concluded, *must* be the *orchestra!*

People continued to stream into the hall amid that unmistakable pre-concert buzz which I knew so well. Listening to conversations around us, we could detect accents from various parts of the country, as well as some from other lands. We couldn't help but notice that most of those around us were much older than either of us, in their fifties, sixties, and then some. It became clear that many of the people were here upon the recommendation of friends who had heard and enjoyed the show during peak season, between April and October.

At precisely 8:00 p.m., the house lights dimmed, leaving the final few guests scurrying into their seats.

*'Ladies and gentlemen, welcome to the Kimball Theatre for a tribute to American music with the 21ˢᵗ Century Orchestra.'*

I looked back up to the control booth but could see no announcer with microphone, so I gathered that this was a prerecorded greeting which served its purpose of quieting the audience.

*'Long after Spike Jones first stumbled onto stage, straddling a comedic concoction of musical gadgets tethered to every bodily appendage, the 21st Century Orchestra invades the stage with laptop computer, digital sound modules, musical instrument digital interface, and an assortment of MIDI controllers. Best of all, this orchestra's drummer never misses the beat, the piano player doesn't smoke three packs-a-day, the bass player doesn't imbibe three pints-a-day, and the brass section never complains about their sore chops!'*

The audience giggled at the humor, and Briggett and I looked at each other, realizing we were all being set up for a very unusual and entertaining evening.

*'And now, please welcome the 21st Century Orchestra.'*

All hands clapped enthusiastically as the evening's casually dressed performer stepped from between the tall curtains at stage center. I could only smile at remembering Woody mention The Performer's long dark curls, generously laced with gray. The Performer smiled warmly, bowed gracefully, and approached the microphone.

"Thank you for coming to the Kimball Theatre this evening," he announced. "It has been my pleasure performing for you...I had a wonderful time...thanks again!"

With that, he turned and began walking back towards the curtain, microphone still in hand. The audience, apparently warned by their friends to expect such vaudevillian, off-the-wall humor, reacted, as expected, uproariously.

"Oh...did I forget something?" he queried as he innocently turned towards the audience once again.

Laughter and guffaws filled the hall. It was obvious this man was comfortable on stage. He had the crowd in his hands before he even played a note of music! That was a technique I wasn't used to, and I made a mental note to remember it, if and when I ever returned to the stage. The thought startled me into the realization that I hadn't even replaced my guitar, which had been lost in the fire at the Ellicott Club. What was I waiting for? Before the people had a chance to quiet down, The Performer picked up what looked like an overgrown clarinet off a small table. I noticed yet another wire running from the bottom of this instrument to the middle of the gear rack. He stepped to the computer hidden within and hit a key with his right index finger, whereupon the rich sounds of a Jazz rhythm section filled the hall. I was stunned at the realism. I strained my eyes, certain the curtains would soon part to reveal the now-hidden pianist, bass player, guitarist, and drummer. But the curtains remained closed. After a four-bar introduction by the still invisible rhythm section, The Performer lifted the strange instrument to his lips and began playing. Although my eyes saw him playing this electrified clarinet-type instrument, my ears heard a mellow muted trumpet. My hair stood on end as I recognized the arrangement of "Misty" as the very same one that Woody and I had performed together. The many strange coincidences leading up to this day put my mind on notice to be wary. But his melodic playing rocked me gently, and I closed my eyes, thinking back to that first set with Woody months ago at the Williamsport hotel. My eyes flew open with a start, as I realized midway through the first chorus that I was indeed listening to Woody's very rendition of this classic song; the same phrasing; the same melodic bursts. It was uncanny.

The Performer abruptly ended his improvisation exactly two bars before the third chorus, which I recognized as the tenor sax player's cue to take the baton, so to speak, with his own *lead-in* to the next chorus.

"Take it, Woody!" The Performer demanded, directing his gaze to the middle of the stage where no one stood.

My heart stopped in mid-beat. There must be an explanation for all this. In the midst of my confusion, the orchestra's tenor saxophonist executed the two-bar lead-in, and was off on his own improvisational journey. Of course, there *was no* tenor saxophonist on stage! The rich, warm tenor sound the audience heard was computerized trickery, but oh, so real. My jaw hit the floor and I felt myself all but paralyzed by the sudden realization that the sax solo I was hearing was the very solo Woody had performed that night with me, note for note! The Performer and his computerized sax soloist proceeded to *trade eights,* which is musical parlance for alternating eight bars each of improvisation over the rhythm section's harmonic foundation. The unseen trumpet section belted out the next chorus, leaving the final one for the muted trumpet soloist to restate the melody. "Misty" closed out with a nice little four-bar coda…precisely the same ending I remember from my own first playing of this song along side Woody.

The audience began clapping appreciatively, and The Performer smiled broadly, then bowed to the continuing applause from the house. I was once again frozen in place, frozen in time, more accurately. I couldn't even raise my arms to support my hands to applaud along with everyone else. I felt myself *drifting,* as the audience finally relented to The Performer's re-grasping of the microphone.

"Hello," he announced.

"Hello!" the audience bellowed in unison.

"Welcome to the Kimball Theatre for A Tribute to American Music. Tell me, how do you like this 21st Century Orchestra?" he asked in jest, sweeping his left arm to indicate the metal rack standing unobtrusively only a few feet from the microphone.

The audience applauded once more, eager to show their approval at what they were hearing. The Performer talked for several minutes about Errol Garner, who had composed "Misty" so many years ago, giving a mini-history lesson with a voice that was as musical sounding as the music itself.

"I'd like to introduce you to the orchestra's first soloist of the evening, whom you just heard playing tenor sax on 'Misty,'" he announced.

With a glimmer in his eyes, hinting at the humor about to be revealed, The Performer continued.

"Please put your hands together for a very gifted and talented young musician...on tenor sax, *Woody Reed!*"

The audience laughed loudly at the absurd humor of a fictitious saxophonist with such an appropriate name...*Woody Reed*...but I couldn't hear a thing. At that moment, the entire concert hall virtually closed in upon me. My heart began to beat much too quickly, my whole body was shaking, and my peripheral vision vanished. I felt in the middle of a dark tunnel, unable to extricate myself from a nightmare growing more obscene by the moment. The Performer was looking right at me, as if a Star Trekkian tractor beam had been cast to irrevocably connect us. He continued speaking to the audience, but I couldn't comprehend the words he was mouthing. It sounded like his voice was lost in an echo chamber, and I gave up even trying to hear his words. All the while, his eyes held mine, by now both of us firmly ensconced within the beam. They were kind eyes, thank goodness, and his expression spoke to me, comforting me, communicating to me, and only me, that he knew who I was, why I was here, and that I shouldn't be afraid. Telepathically, it seemed, I heard his voice in my mind, made all the more confusing by the fact that the words I was hearing didn't match the movements of his lips on stage.

'It's okay, Violetta. You're here for a reason. And you're among friends. Just close your eyes, sit back in your seat, and try not to be afraid. In a moment, I'm going to introduce the next number on the program. When I do, I want you to remember the last time you played this song. It's a song you know well, a song that has deep meaning for you, as it has for Woody. But when you hear the name of this song, don't be alarmed. Just remember: all things happen for a reason. In fact, you've been invited to this very town, on this very weekend, and to this very performance in this hall, tonight. You're not alone, Violetta.'

Suddenly, we were back in real time. I opened my eyes, and The Performer's words now matched the movement of his lips, any trace of echo gone. I felt weak, certain I would pass out, but I repeated his words of comfort to myself, calming my nerves, preparing for what must be coming if he had taken the trouble to warn me of it in advance. I made up my mind at that moment that I would let nothing scare me to the point of losing control of my very thoughts and emotions.

"Thank you so much," he addressed the audience once more. "The next song I'd like to play for you has a bit of history to it, all the way back to 1927, when it was first recorded as a fast, rag-time song. Unfortunately, nobody liked it. In fact, it bombed! So, the composer, a young man by the name of Hoagy Carmichael, came to *me* and asked, '*What do I do now? Nobody likes my song!*'"

As the audience laughed once again, this time at the sheer physical impossibility of Hoagy Carmichael confiding anything to this 50'ish-looking man some 75 years ago, the strangest sensation entered my thoughts. *Could it have been?* I could only wonder. Considering everything else that had already happened to me during the past few months, nothing would have surprised me.

The Performer continued his story for the audience with a teasing smile.

"So I said to him, gee, *I* like your song, Hoagy! It has a wonderful melody. If I were you, though, I'd change it into a ballad. I think you'd have a hit on your hands. Sure enough, given my expert advice, Hoagy re-recorded the song as a ballad, as I suggested, and it ended up becoming the most recorded, most requested song ever written. Of course, you know I'm talking about…'Stardust.'"

While many in the hall showed their anticipation of hearing "Stardust" with an audible '*ahhhh*,' it was all I could do to keep from leaping from my seat and screaming at the top of my voice, '*ENOUGH!*' But I had been warned this was coming, hadn't I? So I followed the advice I had been given, remaining calmly seated, closing my eyes, taking a deep breath, and letting the music lead me to wherever it was I was being led by whomever was leading me there, and for whatever reason. I reminisced to the first time I had played this song with Woody at the Williamsport hotel, then the last time we had played it at the Ellicott Club that fateful night. The Performer was executing a brilliant rendition of "Stardust" on stage, which allowed me to focus on the song, the music, and the mood. I no longer felt scared, but I must admit to a certain wariness in the back of my mind, the feeling enhanced by the beautiful and familiar sound of a tenor sax now emanating from the same instrument that moments ago had sounded like a muted trumpet!

I opened my eyes, looking around me to see women resting their heads on their husbands' shoulders, nostalgically transported to another time in their lives together. And I thought, this is what it's all about, isn't it? What better purpose for music than as a gentle rekindling of emotions so long ago experienced and so deeply enjoyed? The entire experience was exactly as Woody had described it. I suddenly felt very close to him in our common understanding.

Now with a smile on my face, I turned my head again towards the stage, and there he was, this wonderful performer, seemingly encased in the warm amber glow of the spotlights, his body moving to the rhythm of the arrangement as he continued his improvisation.

*'Prepare yourself, Violetta, for what's about to happen will rattle your soul if you allow it to.'*

I sensed him speaking to me as if in a dream. My smile quickly faded, and without further admonition, I saw it with my own two eyes. Had he not warned me in advance, I surely would have run from the hall, screaming like a raving maniac. But then I felt his presence, like Woody's gentle hand on my shoulder, calming me, as a mother would her sick child.

He was...*rising*...from his stage-bound physical body. Without even a hint of the panic I had felt upon my own inability to rise from the confines of this world during my last performance, I turned my head to see if anyone around me was seeing what I was seeing. I couldn't be sure, but no facial expressions changed, no heads were removed from shoulders to follow the ascent, no cries of disbelief were gasped. Indeed, Briggett was still sitting next to me, eyes glued to the performance on stage. I looked forward again to see the spiritual glow now level with the top of the curtain valence. The Performer's body held fast to the stage as the notes flowed from the hall's large concert speakers so expertly hidden behind the valence. Higher and higher the apparition rose, now floating over the top of the hall, no less than 35 feet above the seats. And as I watched and listened, I heard Woody's soulful playing of "Stardust" filling the hall. It seemed to continue for hours, as hands were held, memories were recalled, friendships were remembered, and eyes misted over. In truth, all this occurred within the span of mere minutes, before the glow slowly and gracefully flowed back across the ceiling, back down the curtains, re-entering the body from which it had risen so elegantly.

"Stardust" ended. To say you could hear a pin drop wouldn't even come close to describing the absolute absence of sound, as if sucked from the hall by a giant vacuum. The audience, enraptured, seemed not to want to let go of the moment. But the moment passed, as it always does, and the ensuing applause was as loud and sustained as the moment had been quiet and short. The Performer took a deep bow to acknowledge his appreciation for the audience's reaction, lifting his head in mid-bow to look directly into my eyes. Even from this distance, I saw a tear roll down his cheek, whereupon he bowed his head again.

"Is that not one of the most beautiful songs ever written?" The Performer asked once the audience had quieted down.

"Mmmmm…" was the only response to be heard from the mesmerized crowd.

"With your permission," he added in the most sincere tone, "allow me to dedicate that performance to a very dear and special friend, a musician we all knew as…*Trumpet Man.*"

Woody had told me all about Trumpet Man, his mentor, now deceased for many years. Despite the inner panic I felt, I knew that I had indeed been drawn here for a reason, and I prayed that I would soon be reunited with Woody.

# Chapter Twenty-Nine

*Briggett*

No sooner did we find our seats in the middle of the hall than Violetta began pointing everything out to me, from the balcony behind and above us, to the chandelier hanging from the high ceiling, and the impressive looking rack of electronic gear on stage. I too found myself caught up in the excitement of the moment, taking in all the sights and sounds like a child seeing and hearing her first concert performance. Violetta and I both laughed along with the rest of the audience at the off-the-wall humor employed by The Performer whom Violetta had learned about from Woody. But as the show progressed, I began to notice that Violetta was growing more and more uncomfortable and nervous. I was afraid for her, and I felt the urge to reach over and take her hand in mine to assure her that she wasn't alone. But I also didn't want to interrupt the moment, for I was now convinced that we were both here for a reason, although she more than I, and I felt sure that somehow Woody was central to that reason.

I first sensed something was wrong when The Performer began his rendition of "Misty," indeed the first number in the show. At first, Violetta's eyes were closed as she gently rocked to the rhythm of the music. Then all at once, right in the middle of his solo, she suddenly opened her eyes wide, and I noticed that her hands were actually shaking in her lap. I didn't dare interrupt her thoughts with a question, and I certainly didn't want to disturb those around us who were enjoying the music. But I actually became scared when he later introduced "Stardust," the very song that had been so special for Violetta and Woody. The more The Performer talked to the audience, the more frightened Violetta seemed to become, and the expression on her face could only be described as abject terror. As he began to play his arrangement of this song, I could see Violetta fighting to regain control, to no avail. At one point, she actually turned her head from left to right, and right to left, several times, as if unable to believe that what she was experiencing wasn't being felt by any others in the crowd, including me.

When The Performer played a beautiful tenor sax solo on that strange looking electronic instrument of his, the tears began rolling down Violetta's face uncontrollably. She tilted her head up towards the ceiling, and if I didn't know any better I would have sworn she was following something moving above the stage, unseen to all except her. I wanted so badly to comfort her, but I didn't dare break the spell, and indeed that's what it must have been, for all was certainly beyond the comprehension of my physical senses. I watched her steel her self against all odds, actually clenching her fists tightly to draw upon some inner strength. So I did the only thing I could do. I remained next to her, offering her at least the physical support of knowing I was nearby in case she needed me. Finally, at the conclusion of the sax solo, she actually smiled as if in recognition of some deep meaning that I couldn't know or understand. This was, after all, something she had to go through by herself. I began to feel that she was through the hardest part of the ordeal, and she slumped back in her seat in total exhaustion, her fists unclenching in the process. It was only then that I reached down and took her hand, holding it tightly in my own in the hope that my strength would pass through my hands into hers.

# Chapter Thirty

The Performer maintained mastery of his audience for another hour, taking the crowd not only on a musical journey through the 20<sup>th</sup> Century classic standards of Jazz, but introducing them to the modern world of music technology. Without being professorial, he demonstrated his clarinet-like instrument, which he called an EWI, short for Electronic Wind Instrument, the audience marveling at how easily he could mimic the sound of virtually any orchestral instrument. He talked for a few minutes about the computer's role in his musical world. Upon reaching the final selection of the evening, he solemnly addressed his audience.

"I added this song to my performance repertoire at the end of September, 2001. With everything that's going on in the world today, I invite you to sit in silent contemplation, in the hope this song might stir some emotion within your soul. Or, feel free to stand and join in song. At the conclusion of the show, if you have any questions about the music I've performed tonight, the technology I utilize, or, about life in general, please feel free to wander up to stage front, and I'll answer them to the best of my ability. Thank you again for coming, and good evening."

What followed was the most stirring rendition of "America the Beautiful" I've ever heard. Some people remained in their seats deep in thought. Most, including Violetta and me, stood and joined in song, clapping loudly as the arrangement built through a feverish crescendo, culminating with loud percussive accents from the entire orchestra, especially the brass section. When it was all over, The Performer looked upward, raising his arms as if in supplication, his EWI held high above his head. The audience erupted into thunderous applause now, favoring him with a well-deserved standing ovation and cries of "Bravo!" After savoring the moment, he lowered his arms, placed his instrument back on the table next to the equipment rack, and left the stage the way he had entered.

The crowd continued to applaud as the house lights came back up to full, at which point many satisfied guests began their walk up the aisles, talking excitedly about what they had all just shared. A few dozen others walked down the aisle to stage front, awaiting The Performer's re-entrance to answer their questions. Neither Violetta nor I moved. We *couldn't* move. We had just witnessed the most emotionally draining performance either of us had ever seen, not to mention the spiritual experience which I recognized all too clearly as one Violetta alone had shared with him. I could only sit there soaking it all in. The Performer spent the next half-hour talking with people, answering their questions, laughing, kidding, and even signing an occasional autograph when asked. Through it all, we remained in our seats as if glued, thinking about our journey, wondering what was yet to be revealed.

Once everyone had departed the hall, he walked down the steps from the stage and up the aisle towards us, a serene and knowing look on his face.

"I'm glad you stayed, Violetta," he said, now appearing physically tired from the evening's work.

"Actually...I didn't have much choice...I couldn't move..." she answered with a half smile.

Then, he turned his head and looked right into my eyes. I had the insane feeling he could see deep into my soul, and I experienced a lightheaded sensation.

"I'm glad you're here, too, Briggett," he said so softly that I almost didn't hear him.

"But...how did you...I mean..." I stammered uncontrollably.

"You've been in Woody's thoughts," he whispered.

This time, Violetta grabbed *my* hand, certain I was about to pass out from the shock of the moment.

"Well, I know you both have a ton of questions...but I have only one. Are you hungry?" he asked.

"We're starving," we chimed in unison.

"Just give me a few minutes to pack up my gear, and I'll buy you a sandwich, okay?"

"Only if you let us help you," Violetta offered.

"Deal!" he said, snapping his fingers once.

We three packed his gear into his little Toyota SUV. Violetta and I got in my car and followed him to a restaurant across town. He insisted they had the best grilled-cheese sandwich around. Williamsburg must have been one of those sleepy little towns where they rolled up the sidewalks at 6:00! Here it was, only about 10:00 p.m., and we arrived at the restaurant to claim our choice of empty tables. He virtually collapsed into his chair, now fully giving in to the strain of the evening. A waitress immediately came over and asked if we would like anything to drink before looking over the menu. He looked at her with a straight face.

"I'll have the house ginger ale, please," he said without hinting at a smile.

The waitress also smiled, looking to me, then Violetta, and we both just nodded for the same as she spun on her heels to retrieve our drinks, undoubtedly well used to this one-liner.

"Woody needs our help," he whispered despite the lack of any other people in the dining room. He held Violetta's gaze, not moving an inch. The waitress arrived back at our table with three ginger ales, and asked if we had yet decided on what to order. I hadn't even thought to look at the menu.

"We'll each have a grilled-cheese sandwich," he said, adding, "if that's okay with you, ladies?"

"Sure...that's fine..." we playfully agreed.

"Three peas in a pod," the waitress kidded. "I'll have your orders out shortly."

His eyes were on mine, now, not letting go. I knew what I had to ask, as did he, but I was terrified to let the words escape my mouth, for fear his answer would send Violetta and me into a panic from which we'd never recover. Sensing our fear, he phrased the question for us, saving either of us from having to voice what we knew couldn't be possible.

"You're wondering why you're here, right?" he asked, not once wavering from eye contact.

We could do no more than nod our heads dumbly in agreement. Words just would not come. He went on.

"Woody is lost to us," he said.

Violetta must have known this answer was coming, yet that didn't diminish its impact, like a cold slap in the face. Her eyes were welling with tears, as were mine, with no place to go but down our cheeks and we didn't fight it. He continued speaking in the most gentle and mesmerizing tone.

"Woody is so totally alone, trapped in a time and place not of his own choosing, without even his music to guide him. But he's searching for you even now, as we sit here talking about him. You've been chosen to bring him back, Violetta. And

161

you're the only one who can accomplish that, for you and he share the deepest love and understanding possible. Your journey will be long and difficult. But it must be undertaken, for any further delay puts Woody more at risk of never returning to his rightful place with you."

He gently placed a hand on each of ours across the table.

"It's all right, girls…just let it out. Believe me, I know exactly how you feel. I went through the same revelation many years ago. For the moment, all that matters is that you're here, you've experienced the first step, and you're ready to proceed."

"*Proceed?*" Violetta struggled to ask. "Proceed where?"

"I think you already know the answer to that, don't you?" he asked knowingly, not wanting to upset her any further, if that was even possible.

"Will you…*help* me?" she nearly begged in a strained voice I didn't recognize as hers.

"Of course I will, Violetta. I'll be with you, every step of the way. You see, you've been blessed with The Gift. As I've been blessed. As Trumpet Man was blessed, as Woody was blessed, and all those before us."

"What do I do next?" she asked fearfully.

"The next thing you do is eat your grilled-cheese sandwich!" he smiled, eager to break the feeling of doom we were certainly both experiencing.

At that moment, the waitress brought our sandwich plates, laden with chips and a pickle.

"Anything else I can get you?" she wondered.

"I guess we're all set for now, thanks," he answered on our behalf.

The waitress turned and headed back from where she had come. We ate our sandwiches in silence, knowing that words were irrelevant at this point. When we finished, he ordered cappuccino for each of us. We just sat, and talked about music, about life, and about the reason for us being here.

"It's time, Violetta..." he confided.

"Time for what?" she asked, confused.

"Time to climb back up on the horse," he answered.

"I'm not sure I know what you mean..." she bluffed.

"Did you bring your guitar along with you today, Violetta?" he asked good-naturedly.

I saw Violetta's face turn red with heat.

"I...well...no, I didn't," she answered with no emotion in her voice. "You see...I...haven't touched a guitar since...since the fire destroyed mine months ago...do you know about that, too?"

"Yes, I know. But that doesn't matter. You see," he explained, "I'd like nothing better than for you to sit in with me at tomorrow's matinee performance."

"Sit in? *With you?*" Violetta asked in shocked disbelief.

"Yes, with me," he smiled.

"But *you* know there's no substitute for playing on stage...something I haven't done since the Ellicott Club," she admitted somewhat hesitantly. "And my hands...I just don't know if...if I can..."

He looked directly at her.

"Violetta, it's time to climb back up on the horse. And there's no time like the present, right?"

"I guess so," she mumbled. "To be honest, though, I'm terrified of the thought of what might happen...again..."

"You *should* be!" he said in a joking tone, which totally caught her off guard.

As I sat there, feeling like the odd-girl out, The Performer kept asking her questions.

"Do you know what happened to you that night, Violetta?" he asked. "*You* know, the night you've been trying so hard to forget?"

"I can't say that I *know*, as in knowing that we're sitting here right now, talking about it," she replied slowly, thinking about every word before she verbalized it. "But I *do* know that Woody and I journeyed to a special place…The Zone, he called it, where we were met in the vestibule by Trumpet Man. The second time we traveled there, an inner door was revealed to us. We passed through that door, where I was miraculously reunited with my parents."

I sat there like a fly on the wall, absolutely stunned by what I was hearing. I hadn't a clue what they were talking about, but I began to suspect what had so terrified Violetta during tonight's performance. It was all I could do not to ask questions of my own, but I knew that my role in this play was as yet unexplained. To be honest, I almost dreaded the explanation yet to come for me!

"And the last time?" he prodded firmly.

"The last time…was all wrong," she mouthed while looking off into the distance, shaking her head, searching for deliverance from the pain of that night.

"What was *wrong* about it, Violetta?" he continued quietly but relentlessly.

"It was…forced," she whispered, the words virtually stumbling out of her mouth. "I was selfish, I know that. Woody used to tell me, *'you get there at the right time in the right place with right people for the right reason or you don't get there at all.'* I broke the cardinal rule. *Everything* about that night was *wrong*, but I pushed on for all the wrong reasons. Yet Woody somehow managed to overcome my inability and weakness. He just took over, realizing that I was in no frame of mind to travel with him that night. I was terrified, for he began his ascent without me. And I reached up and out to him, desperately trying to pull him back, which only served to push him away. All I could see were his eyes, fading into the distance above. And then, suddenly, he disappeared in a brilliant flash of blinding white light. My next recollection was waking up in the hospital, my hands and face wrapped in bandages, my memory of that evening blank. Whatever trouble Woody is in, I know it's my fault. And I know I must find him, for if I don't I'll never forgive myself. And I'll never be whole again..."

"And *you*, Briggett?" he asked, turning his head away from Violetta to stare through me like a dagger.

"I'm just a little old waitress!" I exclaimed, drawing Violetta out of her trance into a sudden fit of laughter at the honesty of my response. I suspected he knew I would do that, and actually set me up to accomplish that predetermined task of bringing Violetta back to reality. I was beginning to feel like a puppet on a string. At first, I didn't care for the feeling. But once I gave into it, I found it quite enjoyable, like not having a care in the world. I went with the flow.

He smiled warmly at me. Indeed, the warmth of his smile was like sitting in front of a hot fire on a cold evening, and it felt wonderful.

"You may consider yourself less than you really are, Briggett," he went on, "but you play a very important role in the outcome of this journey."

"I do?" I asked stupidly.

"Yes, you do," he answered. "Consider yourself the missing link, or, more accurately, the missing piece of a puzzle. Without you, the rest of the pieces don't fit, indeed, *can't* fit. *With* you, though, the final picture presents itself in its totality. Without you, Violetta could never have come this far. And without you again, her journey will end here, as will Woody's. So you see, a tremendous burden has been placed upon you. To put it another way, you've been chosen for this task by powers you can never comprehend. But you *have* been chosen, like it or not. I see in you a strength of character you never knew you had, and a compassion that makes you the only choice for helping Violetta and Woody."

I sat there, looking from him to Violetta and back to him, wondering how I had ever been cast in this drama being played out before my very eyes. And yet, despite the gravity of his words, I wasn't afraid. I knew I *was* the link to reuniting Woody and Violetta, though I had no idea why or how, and I was determined not to let either of them down. And at that moment, I knew that this man sitting before me already knew the outcome yet to unfold.

"I'm ready," I said calmly.

"I know you are, Briggett," he answered. "And you, Violetta?"

"Yes…I'm ready, too," Violetta said with conviction in her soft voice. "But…I don't even have a guitar to play…"

"You leave that little detail to me, young lady!" he joked. "Let's just say I'm owed a favor or two by a local music professor. You just be at the rear stage door tomorrow, ready to do your thing, no later than 1 o'clock, okay?"

"Okay…and…thank you," Violetta managed.

At that, the three of us stood to leave, marching out of the restaurant with our arms around each other's shoulder, with The Performer between Violetta and me. I guess we must have looked like the Three Musketeers, but so what! We were the only people in the place, other than the waitresses and the cashier. And they sure didn't seem to mind.

Once outside, he got in his car, waved, and turned left for home. Briggett and I just stood there, looking at each other in disbelief not only because of the conversation we had just had, but because we both realized at the same instant that we had never bothered to check into a motel for the night. So there we stood, two statues, laughing at ourselves, before we finally got into my car and turned right to search for a motel that Violetta remembered Woody telling her about.

# Chapter Thirty-One

*Thomas*

I checked my email when I got home from work at the hotel, surprised, and delighted, to see another message from Woody Reed.

*Thomas: I almost forgot! I suspect the person with Violetta that day was, indeed, a friend of mine named Briggett. Yes, she is a waitress I've known for years. She works at a restaurant on Park Avenue in Rochester called the Frog Pond. Do yourself a favor. Go visit her. I'm sure she'll remember you. Trust me, it's never too late. I know in my heart you two should be together, Thomas.*

*Later,*
*Woody*

# Chapter Thirty-Two

*Violetta*

Only a few blocks after turning onto Richmond Road, Briggett and I found the little bungalow-style motel Woody had told me about. Briggett waited in the car while I went into the office to ask for a room for the night. I rang the old style bell on the counter, and it took several minutes for the clerk to emerge from behind a curtain at the rear of the office. He looked like ten miles of bad road, and I suddenly realized I had probably awakened him from a deep sleep on a cot bed in the back room. Within thirty seconds, I had the key to a bungalow at the back of the property. Exhausted from the long drive, not to mention the events of the day, we both fell asleep as soon as our heads hit our pillows. My last conscious thought before falling into that deep sleep was about tomorrow's show; what would happen, whether I was ready to perform, and if I would ever see Woody again.

For some reason, my dreams began to take a very strange twist. I was thinking to myself how strange this twist was as I was experiencing the dream, like being two people looking at something at the same time but not being able to tell each other about it. Lenny Dee flashed into my dream, and I was thrown back to being rescued by him from the Ellicott Club fire. I realized I was thrashing in bed, and mumbling out loud, spiraling down into a deep hole, when all at once I became aware that something was shaking me from my sleep. I awoke with a start. My eyes flew open. My heart was pounding thunderously in my chest, threatening to escape my body. Briggett had apparently been shaking me from my nightmare, and her hand was still on my shoulder when I thrust myself up into a sitting position in bed, sweat pouring down my face.

"Violetta, Violetta," she kept repeating until my senses took over. "Wake up, you're having a nightmare...wake up!"

I sat there, my eyes glued to hers. Although awake, I felt in a daze. And as I looked at her, my imagination took over my thoughts. And then, as if in a trance, I began to repeat my thoughts out loud as they were occurring in my mind.

"Lenny...Leonardo...Lenny...Leo...Dee...Divencenzo...Lenny Dee...Leonardo Divencenzo...oh my God, Briggett..."

Briggett could do nothing more than sit there and stare at me in total disbelief. After what seemed like hours later but could only have been minutes, she reached out and took both my hands in her own.

"Well, V," she intoned. "I guess we now know why I was invited along on this journey, don't we?"

# Chapter Thirty-Three

*Woody*

I arrived at the rear stage door to find it had been left ajar, anticipating my arrival. As I entered, Emma Jane was waiting inside. When she saw me, she gave me a warm hug before speaking.

"Are you ready, Woody?" she asked.

"Ready is my middle name, Emma Jane!" I joked to relieve my nervousness.

"Woody Ready Reed? *That's* a funny name!"

I just shook my head at that one, thankful for the return humor, corny or not.

"How about if you take a few minutes to warm up in the dressing room, Woody, while we finish setting up, okay?"

"Sure thing," I mumbled.

This was a routine I was used to. I walked into the dressing room behind stage. It looked exactly like I remembered it from 25 years ago. The only differences were fresh paint and new furniture, but otherwise nothing had changed. I took my sax out of its burgundy velvet-lined case and proceeded to immerse myself in a series of warm-up exercises to loosen up my fingers, not to mention my thoughts. Once comfortable, I put the sax down and did a few deep breathing exercises to give me access to a wind player's greatest asset in performance, that being breath control.

Before I knew it, I heard a knock on the door. I opened it to find Emma Jane smiling at me, beckoning me to the stage for our sound check. The theater's digital sound system was awesome, filling the hall with the rich sounds of our little musical tests. Once we got the sound down, I stood for a few moments and looked out at the hall, exactly as I had done 25 years ago. It's funny how the perspective from the stage is so dramatically different from that of sitting in the audience. The stage was wide and raised, looking out over the 400 seats arranged in perfect symmetry. Unless you've ever performed on stage, I can't think of the words to describe the feeling of a theater you're about to perform in. In a word, it's magical. I looked up to the left to see the balcony I remembered from my first visit here, getting a friendly thumbs-up from the sound and lighting director, who pressed the button on his talk-back microphone.

"You guys ready?" he asked.

Emma Jane, Caden Michael, and Chelsea Miranda all looked at me, as if asking the same question themselves. I nodded, returning the thumbs-up to the balcony.

"Okay, then, time for you four to disappear so we can let the house in," the director replied.

With that, we walked back through the curtains to await the beginning of our performance a few minutes from now. We sat down back stage, and Emma Jane patted me on the knee before speaking.

"The hardest part for you, Woody, will be the opening. Just leave it to us. We'll go out first and warm up the audience before I call you out, so be ready. Trust me, by the time I introduce you, they'll already be in the palm of your hand," she said encouragingly, bringing back a memory of the first time I had heard that very promise offered by her Papa.

My nerves must have been showing, and Caden recognized it right away, clapping me on the shoulder a couple of times as he said the four words I needed to hear at that moment.

"Just have fun, Woody!"

Chelsea smiled at me, clapping her hands in front of her as if to applaud the show about to be delivered. She winked slyly, and the three of them stepped through the curtains to the thunderous applause of the audience as if leaping into a different physical dimension on the other side of the curtain. There I sat on *my* side of the curtain…the *back* side…feeling so totally alone and out of place. Years ago, The Performer had started his show with a quick little joke before jumping right into the first selection. But for this performance, Emma Jane did something different, addressing her audience without humor at the outset.

"Thank you, friends! Welcome to the Kimball Theatre this evening. Let me tell you, you're all in for a *special* treat tonight. A little later on, a very talented and gifted musician will be sitting in with us on tenor sax. Believe me, when you hear him play, you'll understand just how great he is. But first…*let's rock-and-roll!*"

The rafters of this old theater shook as they kicked off the show with a high-energy medley of their own hit songs, music that was unfamiliar to me but obviously well known and loved by their audience. Peeking through the curtains, I soon realized I was indeed observing three masterful musicians and performers, despite their youth. They paced their show perfectly, bringing the audience up, then letting them down ever so gently before bringing them back up higher than the time before. I was feeling elated, not to mention warm, happy, satisfied, fulfilled…*at home*. Mostly, though, I couldn't wait to get out onto that stage. About thirty minutes into the show, I got up and started pacing back and forth behind the curtain, breathing deeply, preparing myself for what was to come. And then, I heard Emma Jane on stage introducing the next number.

"Well, I told you that you were in for a real treat tonight, and the time is *now!* Please welcome a most gifted performer who played on this very stage a quarter of a century ago with our own Papa…on tenor saxophone, Mr. Woody Reed!"

At that moment, my heart dropped into my stomach. I felt as if I would faint from the overwhelming nervousness I was attempting to conquer after all I'd been through in the past days, when I suddenly realized that it had indeed been 25 years since I had last performed here! Somewhat bolstered by the thought that if I could get through it *then*, I could certainly get through it *now*, I squeezed through the closed curtains. The three of them were silhouetted in the bright spotlight at stage front, Emma Jane's right arm raised in my direction to welcome me to my spot on stage. The biggest, warmest smiles on all their faces sure helped to calm my nerves, and I realized that I was skipping across the stage like a little kid!

A full house of people applauded my entrance, apparently convinced that if Emma Jane *said* I was good, then I must *be* good! I took my first bow of the evening, head down, absorbing the karma from the audience, so grateful that Emma had done exactly as she had promised by putting them in the palm of my hand before I had even played a note of music. Emma Jane's introduction of the next song floored me. In truth, we hadn't even thought to discuss what songs we might play together, but I should have known what was about to come.

"Heyyy, you've been a *great* audience tonight, and we've had a blast playing for you! We'd like to play this next song for Woody, and you're about to hear why! This tune has a history going back to *1927*," she said with a hint of incredulity. "Think about that...100 years! Most of you have probably never heard of this song, because it was written way back before your *great-great-grandparents* were born! What can I tell you? I'm a sucker for old Jazz standards, which is what this song is."

She turned her head towards me and asked, "D'you know 'Stardust,' Woody?"

I smiled ear to ear, eerily transported back to the first time I had been asked that very question by Trumpet Man on my first gig as a twelve-year-old.

"You start, I'll jump in!" I said elatedly.

The audience chuckled and began to applaud, more in appreciation of my enthusiastic reaction than in anticipation of hearing me perform, but that didn't bother me a bit. I felt an overwhelming rush of emotion, and a desperate eagerness to play this song in my own way in this place on this day at this time.

Chelsea Miranda spoke to the audience next.

"We know that this song has special meaning for Woody, ladies and gentlemen. So please, sit back, listen up, and prepare to be enthralled with the *hippest* rendition of 'Stardust' you'll *ever* hear!"

Caden Michael kicked it off on percussion with a deliciously slow Chicago blues-style beat, taking me back to the first time I had traveled to The Zone so many years ago while filling in for a sick member of a fusion rock band. Chelsea and Emma soon joined in playing electric guitar and violin, all three of them backed up by their pre-programmed electronic bass and keyboard riffs. As for me, I did what I seemed to do best, filling in as tastefully as I could behind their lead. These kids could sure *cook*, and "Stardust" built in intensity from chorus to chorus, bringing the audience to their feet more than once with driving back-beats. We were having a grand old time, we were! And then, at the point in this song that had long ago become my secret pass-key to The Zone, I ambled up to the microphone at stage front and prepared myself to blast off into my solo cadenza. As I did, the three of them abruptly stopped playing, that being my cue. As I raised my horn to my lips, I heard Emma Jane's voice behind me.

"Take it, Woody!"

And I did. Those three words were music to my ears yet again. I mean, it felt so good, so right, that I just let it all hang out, as they say. I was wailin', no doubt about it. Without me even realizing it, the three of them ever so quietly left the stage, stepping back through the curtains through which I had just entered. Under any other circumstances, I might have been jolted by such a surprise, but not on this night. Everything felt so...*right*. And I realized that this was their gift to me, as it had been their Papa's gift to me so many years ago. There could be no more generous gesture from one musician to another. This was, after all, their audience, their show. What greater compliment than to turn both over to me so unselfishly?

As they must have suspected would happen, I was immediately caught up in the moment, offering the audience my own soulful solo cadenza that I had played years earlier at Trumpet Man's funeral. Eyes closed, I tuned out all evidence of a reality other than that of my playing. I was so intently focused on the moment that a tornado could have swirled across the stage and I wouldn't even have noticed a breeze. As I played, I could see Violetta's eyes in my mind, pleading, locking onto my soul. All the while, I understood that my thoughts were once again splitting into two halves, one side concentrating on the music emanating from my mind at this moment in time, the other on the emotional impact the music would soon exert on my senses.

That realization brought with it the familiar sensation of *seeing* the red glow of the spotlight through my tightly closed eyelids, simultaneously feeling the tears rolling down my cheeks. I knew what was coming, as Emma, Caden and Chelsea must have known I would. I even smiled to myself at the thought of them walking off the stage so purposefully, so stealthily, secure in their knowledge of what was about to happen. I didn't fight it. I just kept thinking about Violetta, how much I loved her, and how I much I needed to be with her again.

Then, it happened. I experienced the *rising* from the confines of my physical body still tethered to the stage floor. I felt myself floating up the curtains to the ceiling, the hall so far below, over an audience completely unaware of what was taking place in a dimension obviously beyond the scope of their sensory recognition or spiritual comprehension. I was looking down at myself as my body maintained the necessary physical posture of a saxophonist wailing both on and through his instrument. Then I felt it, that brush against my arm that I so vividly remembered. On this occasion, I welcomed it, calling out a thought from my inner mind.

'*Trumpet Man, is that you?*'

'*Hey, kid,*' I heard through a cold rush in my ear. '*Welcome back!*'

Those simple words put me at ease with myself, and I made up my mind to remain in this place for as long as I could, or perhaps as long as I would be allowed. Soaking warmth surrounded me as if I was being embraced. Of course, *embrace* is only a word, a tool of language wholly insufficient to describe what I was experiencing. I realized again that I would never be able to relate this re-entrance to anyone who hadn't been here, because there were no words in any language I knew of that approached an adequate description of something that wasn't even known to exist.

I experienced fully this welcome reminder of the implausible yet seemingly apparent existence of parallel dimensions. After all, far down below I could still see and hear myself performing "Stardust," despite the fact…for it must *be* a fact…that I was indeed engaged in this other-worldly communication with someone who no longer was a part of my physical world below. I literally broke out laughing at the mere thought of my thought! Trumpet Man actually joined me in laughter, which was so absurd it made me laugh all the more.

*'Wild ride, isn't it, Woody?'* he managed to ask between laughs.

*'Wild doesn't even begin to describe it,'* I replied.

Through our laughter, I sensed a rectangular-shaped glow straight ahead of me, shimmering in my vision. Of course, telling you all this is so difficult, because, as I've already mentioned, there is no such thing as *rectangle,* or *straight ahead,* or *shimmering.* The best I can do is try to explain to you that it didn't appear as a two-dimensional box, but rather a three-dimensional form, with infinite depth, and no apparent end in sight.

*'Door number one!'* Trumpet Man bellowed, exactly as he had done so many years ago.

Once again, I burst into hearty laughter. The absurdity of his *door number one* television reference was just too much to handle, made all the more so by his own joking and laughing, which helped me remember that this was indeed a beautiful place.

'*Where are doors number two and three?*' I asked in a smirking tone of thought.

'*I should have known you'd ask that, Woody! But one door at a time is all you get!*'

'*Okay…so…what's behind door number one?*' I asked again, just as I had done years ago on another journey.

He replied, '*Only one way to find out, Woody. Step right in…I mean, through.*'

To quit now would constitute the ultimate cop-out. I closed my eyes, despite the fact that there was nothing here to see anyway, and willed my thoughts to propel me through the door, or, whatever it was. Sure enough, before I knew what had happened, I believe I must have successfully passed through the doorway, because it disappeared from my thoughts in a brilliant flash of white light.

# Chapter Thirty-Four

*Violetta*

Briggett and I spent the rest of the night talking, preparing ourselves for what we hoped to happen this day. We spent the hours calming each other down from the shock of the realization that *my* Lenny Dee and *her* Leonardo Divencenzo was indeed one and the same person. This could be no coincidence, we well understood. Imagine, Lenny being my appointed guardian, and Leo being hers, as well, not to mention her uncle! It defied rationalization, to say the least. But it also served to give us insight to the special bond of friendship that we had so quickly established. *'Everything happens for a reason, though we may never know the reason,'* we reminded ourselves.

Unable or unwilling to sleep any more, we showered and headed out to breakfast. Neither of us said a word the entire time we fortified our bodies with pancakes and coffee. Words had become unnecessary to our mission. At one o'clock sharp, we parked her car behind the Kimball Theatre. The rear stage door had been left ajar, as if anticipating our arrival. As soon as we entered, The Performer greeted us both with a warm smile and a hug.

"Wait here, I have a little surprise for you," he said to me with a wink.

As he turned and walked over to the dressing room, Briggett and I looked at each other, wide-eyed, wondering what surprise could possibly top the surprises of this journey. He returned carrying something large enough to be cumbersome, yet small enough to be covered by a blanket.

"For you, Violetta," he said seriously as he removed the blanket.

And there, before my eyes, was my guitar. No, I don't mean a guitar *like* the one I had lost in the fire. I mean *my guitar*. I was sure of it. I was about to burst into tears.

"But...*how*..." I stuttered, unable to find the right words.

"Don't ask," he answered with mock seriousness. "Let's just say you're not alone, Violetta."

With that, he led me into the dressing room and suggested I take the time necessary to reacquaint myself with my guitar, at the same time gesturing to Briggett with his eyes that she leave me alone and join him on the stage to set up for this afternoon's show. She happily and eagerly complied.

I retreated to the dressing room. Sitting down, I had no way of knowing if this was, in fact, my own guitar, or if it was merely another similar guitar. I reminded myself that mine had indeed burned up in the fire months ago at the Ellicott Club. But as I began to caress notes from it, any doubts as to its authenticity were quickly erased. It felt too perfect, too *right* in my hands and to my ears. It didn't take me long to settle into a kind of conversation with my fingers, coaxing them back to musicality and flexibility. And as my digits returned to form, so too did my voice, which I had used for nothing but talking of late. I reveled in the thought that music was within me, and it would take more than mere blood, sweat and tears to stifle this gift. I found myself thinking of Woody...and Briggett...and The Performer...and everyone and everything else I had encountered on my journey thus far. And then there was a soft knock on the dressing room door. I took a deep breath, got up, and opened the door.

"Ready, Violetta?" he asked in a whisper.

"Ready," I answered.

He led me to a place behind the curtain where I would await his call to join him on stage. Despite the heavy curtains blocking my view, I could hear the loud buzz of anticipation in the audience out there, on the other side of the curtains, awaiting his entrance. Before stepping through the curtains, he turned back to me for a moment.

"We've got some work ahead of us, Violetta. But just follow my lead. I won't let anything bad happen to you," he promised. "Leave everything to me, I'll call out each song for you. I have no doubt you'll know all of them. That's the beauty of playing the old standards...*every*body knows them!"

"Okay," I agreed. "But I don't mind telling you, I'm a nervous wreck! This is the first time I'll be stepping on stage since the fire...you just might have to pick me up off the floor."

He chuckled.

"Nervous is good, Violetta. It shows you care. Believe me, the nervousness will pass as soon as you play the first note of the first song. Most important, though, is to relax. Don't push. Just let the music happen naturally. Your goal here today should be nothing more than getting comfortable in the music again, and comfortable on the stage. Anything more is a bonus."

*'And now, please welcome the 21ˢᵗ Century Orchestra!'*

He smiled at me, winked, and stepped through the curtains to the loud applause of the audience, as if leaping into a different physical dimension on the other side. There I sat on my side of the curtains, feeling so totally alone and out of place.

"Thank you, ladies and gentlemen," he began. "Welcome to the Kimball Theatre this afternoon for A Tribute to American Music with the 21st Century Orchestra. Let me tell you, you're all in for a *special* treat today. Two for the price of one, because a very talented young musician will be sitting in with me this afternoon. And when you hear her sing and play the guitar, you'll understand just how great she's destined to become. Please, give a warm Williamsburg welcome to my young friend, direct from an engagement at the Ellicott Club in Rochester, New York: Violetta!"

I timidly squeezed through the closed curtain to see him silhouetted in the bright spotlight at stage front, his right arm raised in my direction to welcome me to my spot on stage. But he didn't wait for me to join him. No, he walked back to me, took my elbow in support, and helped me to my chair at stage front, obviously not wanting me to have to even think about tripping as I had done that night at the Ellicott Club. As we walked, I could only wonder to myself how he could have known about that fall. When I was seated comfortably, the biggest, warmest smile on his face sure helped to calm my nerves. I looked out to see a full house of people applauding my entrance, apparently convinced that if he *said* I was good, then I must *be* good! And there was Briggett in the front row, giving me the thumbs up for encouragement. Strange, I thought to myself, but this would be the first time Brig had ever heard me perform.

I took my first bow of the afternoon, the first of many, it would turn out. Without wasting another moment, or even bothering to see if I was ready, The Performer launched us into the first song, Billy Strayhorn's "Lush Life." I had to laugh to myself, and I'm sure a smile was visible on my face, for this was precisely how I had challenged Woody that first night on the stage at the hotel in Williamsport! "Lush Life" is not a song for the novice. First of all, it's not a song known to most people, let alone to the average musician. Secondly, it's not an easy song to play. The chord progression is, how shall I say, most unique and nonstandard, convincing me that The Performer intended to put me to the test right from the get go, just as I had tested Woody. As he played the melody above his computerized pre-programmed instrumental accompaniment, I ever so gently wove my answering guitar phrases around his rich tenor sax sound, always allowing him adequate space to express himself without worrying about what I was playing behind him. By the middle of the first chorus, I could see that he was appreciating the sensitivity of my musical answers to his instrumental impressions, and his smile virtually lit up the stage. Then, he turned his head slightly towards me, indicating that I should now '*take it,*' without his having to tell me so in words.

Undaunted and completely at home within the unusual harmonic structure of "Lush Life," I took us on a meandering little ride through the wonderful mind of composer Billy Strayhorn before surrendering the stage back to The Performer. There was no need to worry about how to end the song, for the best ending is the most natural one, which we employed without forethought. As I held my last note, eyes closed, he *whispered* one final saxophone flourish around me. When finished, we both had no choice but to remain in place, eyes still closed, savoring the moment, tasting the richness of our first creative encounter. Only after several cherished seconds had passed did I open my eyes and look up at him, realizing that our musical interplay had been virtually the same as what I had enjoyed with Woody that first night. It was uncanny, but I felt like I was on stage with two different people beside me.

He began playing the introduction to the next song before the audience had ceased their applause for the previous one. Once again, as had happened on stage with Woody, Harold Arlen's "Stormy Weather" provided a wonderful showcase for me to display my raunchy, blues side, bending my guitar strings to the delight of all. We followed next with Cole Porter's classic "What Is This Thing Called Love," Walter Gross's "Tenderly," and finally George Gershwin's "Someone To Watch Over Me." I could only wonder if the people in the audience had even the slightest idea that they were witnesses to a virtual repeat performance on stage in front of their eyes. Regardless, the audience sensed they were fortunate to bear witness to our creative exchanges, and he turned to me as he prepared to announce the final selection of the show, eager for me to share in the joy he was unafraid to display at our performance.

"Ladies and gentlemen, I'd like to thank you for spending your time with us this afternoon. I must say, this has been a truly special day for me. Please show your appreciation to our guest artist today, a very special guitarist and singer, Violetta."

The audience stood and applauded enthusiastically for several minutes. Despite my attempts to coax them back into their seats, they would having nothing to do with that, serenading us with unabashed affection in the only way they knew how.

"Thank you again," he smiled, not waiting for them to quiet down. "With your kind permission, we'd like to perform one more beautiful old standard for you."

The Performer turned his eyes towards me, and these three words floated across the stage.

"You know 'Stardust?'"

You can well imagine what was running through my mind as I pondered his query. My first thought was of Woody. I was next overwhelmed by recollections of my last performance at the Ellicott Club, when my selfish actions seemed to have ignited a chain reaction that was beyond my worst nightmare. Did The Performer have an insight that I couldn't dare imagine? Or was this yet another coincidence in a growing list of coincidences that were giving new shape to my existence?

"It's…my favorite song," I whispered while holding his kind gaze intently, almost oblivious to the presence of anybody other than the two of us.

"Then why don't you begin, Violetta? I'd love to hear you play and sing this song in your own way. I'll just back you up on tenor sax," he said softly.

With only the slightest of nods, I closed my eyes and eased into the wonderful and touching introduction to "Stardust," ever so gracefully caressing the chords from my guitar while mouthing words that had been so beautifully crafted many years before.

# Chapter Thirty-Five

*The Performer*

On the spur of that moment, I decided not to play at all during the introduction, content to listen and watch as those in the audience were doing, taking in the full impact of Violetta's gift. Once she entered the first verse, I began weaving gentle tenor saxophone flourishes around her voice, balancing her musical phrases with my own. As we reached the second verse, she signaled me with her eyes to assume the lead role in our duet. I had absolutely no doubt that my refusal to take the lead wouldn't upset her the least bit. Indeed, she welcomed the invitation I was about to offer before I even offered it, undoubtedly hoping that she would have the opportunity to make her own way to wherever it was she was headed.

"Take it, Violetta," I said from off to her side. "This one's all yours."

Violetta calmly and gratefully picked up on my cue, taking full musical advantage of the total freedom to soar as high and as far as she could have wished for without concern for any rhythmic or harmonic constraints from me. Once she realized my plan for her cadenza, she obliged me by giving in to the moment, thrusting herself into a dazzling cascade of guitar virtuosity built upon raw emotion. As naturally as one could imagine, she soon began mimicking her guitar's melodic lines with her voice, note for note, without faltering. I could only smile, seeing her laugh to herself as her improvisations grew in scope beyond any structured confines of "Stardust." And as she continued to find the lovely humor in this most unusual musical interplay with herself, I knew she was at the threshold of splitting her thoughts between the music and her thoughts *about* the music, propelling her even further into the stratosphere. I knew, as did she, what was coming. And I could see that she was totally prepared for the journey this time, unafraid of where it would lead her, content that she was doing it for the right reasons, at the right time, with the right people.

I saw her out-of-body ascent from the stage as Violetta's inner glow began its rise, the audience oblivious to what was taking place right in front of their eyes yet unseen to them. But looking down into the front row, I saw Briggett's mouth open wide in amazement, her eyes following Violetta's ascent up the curtain to the ceiling above. Not surprisingly, Briggett gasped, cupping her fingers in front of her face, looking from side to side to see if anyone else in the audience was seeing what she was seeing. When she realized that she alone was privy to Violetta's long awaited journey to The Zone, she sank back into her chair, resting her head as far back on the seat as possible. She knew what was happening before her very eyes, and she wasn't going to miss a moment of it.

As the brilliant musical improvisation continued to flow uninterrupted from her guitar and voice, Violetta looked downward, basking in the realization that Briggett was able to visualize her ascent. And then, there was a brilliant flash of white light.

# Chapter Thirty-Six

*Woody*

I felt myself propelled at unworldly speed through time and space, vision a mere blur. The first time I had experienced this sensation after my ascent from the Ellicott Club's stage that fateful night, I was terrified, lost in the fear of my unknown direction and destination. But this time, I fully embraced the moment, convinced I was on my way to the place and time in which I belonged. As my aura began its descent, I realized with a start that I was returning not to the Kimball Theatre, but to the Ellicott Club's stage, where I saw Violetta's beautiful green eyes below me. To my surprise, her arm was still raised in search of my return. But as soon as she caught sight of my eyes, her demeanor changed, and once more she immersed her soul into the performance of her own music on stage, focusing solely on the moment. My descent slowed dramatically and suddenly, the blur in my peripheral vision emerging into clear focus. There, on the stage next to Violetta below me, was my physical self still wrapped up in the cascades of emotion emanating from my saxophone. As I hovered close to the ceiling, I saw Lenny Dee, standing off to one side of the audience. His look of panic upon my earlier departure immediately changed to overwhelming joy as he saw my return, his arthritic hands once again steepled in front of his face, his eyes following the slow descent of my aura down the curtain. Then, as suddenly as it had begun, I was back on stage in the moment, Violetta at my side.

# Chapter Thirty-Seven

*Violetta*

I felt myself floating above the stage. As my aura began its descent, I realized with a start that I was returning not to the Kimball Theatre, but to the Ellicott Club's stage. Oblivious to any fear I might have felt...indeed *should* have felt at such a realization, I fully embraced the moment, convinced I was on my way to the place and time in which I belonged. To my surprise, my arm was still raised in search of his return, as it had been that fateful night. But as soon as I saw Woody, still immersed in the performance of his music on the stage, I lowered my arm back to my guitar, whereby my descent slowed dramatically and suddenly, my vision emerging into clear focus. There, on the stage next to Woody, was my physical self, once again immersed in the cascade of emotion emanating from my guitar. And there, standing off to the side of the audience, I saw Lenny Dee, his panic stricken expression replaced by a look of thankfulness, his arthritic hands now steepled in front of his face, his eyes following the slow descent of my aura down the curtain. Then, as suddenly as it had begun, I was back on stage in the moment, Woody at my side.

# Chapter Thirty-Eight

*Woody*

Back in real time, in this moment, with Violetta at my side once again, there was no gasping for breath down on my knees. There was no desperate searching for where I was, how I'd arrived here, and what had happened. No, I knew exactly where, when, why, and with whom I was now sharing this stage. Past confusion was replaced by the security of *feeling* that I had arrived at my destination in the right way, at the right time, with the right person, and for the right reasons. Much to my own surprise, I was calm, able to fully absorb the richness of it all.

Looking at Violetta seated next to me on stage, her eyes told the same story. The music complete, she lifted herself from her chair with a sense of wonderment on her face, and we embraced, she managing to hold her guitar in her left hand, me holding my sax in mine. All the while, our audience applauded and cheered incessantly, eager to show their appreciation for the performance they had just witnessed, yet could never fully comprehend. She and I continued our embrace for what must have seemed like years to some! Finally, we turned towards the audience, each of us with one arm around the back of the other, our instruments held out on each side of us. We bowed once, slowly and most appreciatively. We retreated from the stage, but could not escape the adulation of those before us, walking back out several times to acknowledge the continuing applause. We both knew we should perform an encore. But we both also realized all too clearly that we had traveled long and far to reach this destination. The oppressive need for the restorative and recuperative sleep was particularly strong, draining our energy reserves by the moment.

There would be no encore this night. Rather, we gave one final wave to the audience, helped each other walk off the stage, and signaled the director to close the curtains. We retreated to the dressing room back stage, nearly collapsing as we entered. It took all our strength and endurance to pull the two couches together to form one large enough for us to sleep on. With no gas left in our tanks, we crawled under an afghan blanket fully dressed, literally passing out in each other's arms within seconds.

# Chapter Thirty-Nine

*Violetta*

I woke up to the realization that my eyes were searching for something, anything familiar about my surroundings. It was pitch black. Yet I didn't have the sense that it was nighttime. I felt wide-awake. But there was something else. There was an arm draped around my shoulder. Indeed, I felt that I was in bed with someone, which startled me to a full sitting position in an instant.

"What?" he muttered in confusion.

At that moment I realized I was with Woody. I couldn't see his face in the dark, but I knew it was he. I felt him get up, and after a stumble or two followed by a couple of grunts of frustration, he had obviously managed to find the light switch, for we were now bathed in bright light from the one overhead fluorescent bulb in the middle of the ceiling. We looked at each other, then around the room at our surroundings.

"Good morning, Violetta," he said softly as he had done each morning leading to today.

"It certainly is, Woody," I answered, trying to hide the confused look on my face, for I had no idea where we were or how we had ended up here.

Woody's eyes did a quick turn around the room before he returned his gaze to me and pushed his hair out of his eyes with his right hand.

"That must have been one heck of a show last night, Violetta," he half kidded. "'Only problem is, I can't remember a thing about it!"

Although my eyes remained glued to his, my mind turned inward. I spoke before I even had a thought about saying anything.

"The Ellicott Club," I whispered. "We're in the dressing room, Woody."

"That we are," he agreed, not at all convinced of the fact.

Woody got up slowly, opened the door, and peered out into an empty hallway. Only as he began to close the door did he see the note taped to its front. He removed the note, closed the door, and read the written message aloud.

*Great show last nite, youse two! You really out dun your last show by a mile, and dat's sayin' sumptin'. Talk to youse later. T'day is Sunday…sleep late, da place'll be empty all day. Maybe youse could even go to church, ya know? Couldn' hurt…*
*Lenny*

The clock on the counter told the story. It was 1:45. It was only then that we looked at each other…*really* looked…to notice that we were both fully dressed in clothes rumpled from sleeping in them. A quick mental calculation on my part indicated that we had slept more than sixteen hours, since we had concluded our show by about 9:30 last night.

"We must have traveled far and long last night, Woody," I said, attempting to piece together what neither of us seemed able to remember.

Woody had a confused look on his face, as if he was trying to focus on something that was just out of touch.

"I know there's something we're supposed to be doing today, Violetta. For the life of me, though, I can't put my finger on it!"

He slowly sat back down on the sofa next to me, his eyes wandering to the clock, now reading 1:52.

"Oh, my gosh," he blurted out loudly. "We're supposed to be over at Cassie's house by 3 o'clock, Violetta! We promised her we'd visit today, remember? How could I have forgotten that? If I don't make it there this time, she'll never forgive me! Quick...do you have a quarter?"

I fumbled around in my purse, which I found in the hidden pouch inside my guitar case. I found a quarter and handed it to Woody. He scrambled back out into the hallway, half running to the pay phone on the wall. Without a second thought, he dialed the number as if it was one he dialed every day, though I knew it wasn't. And that caused me a momentary feeling of...oh, I don't know...confusion. I knew we had made this appointment to visit Cassie and her family today, but something deep down just didn't connect in my memory. And as quickly as it had entered my mind, the thought vanished, and I heard Woody concluding his conversation.

"Okay, Cassie...we'll be there as soon as we can...I know, I know...I'm sorry. We had a big show last night at the club and we just managed to crawl out of bed a few minutes ago...thanks...yes, we'll be there by 3:30 at the latest...we wouldn't miss it for the world...okay, see you in a few, Cassie."

We took a fast and unsatisfying shower together before throwing our rumpled clothes back on. By 2:30 we had loaded all our stuff into Woody's car, for we had left my bus at his apartment last night, planning to sleep there after the show. The entire way over to Cassie's house, Woody didn't say a word.

Nor did I. Every time I looked at him, he seemed to be deep in concentration. Finally, we pulled into Cassie's driveway. Woody turned off the ignition and slowly turned towards me.

"What's wrong, Woody?" I asked.

"I don't know, Violetta. Something just feels…out of place or something," he answered with that look of indecision taking over his normally certain facial expression.

"Me, too, Woody," I whispered, looking out the car window to see a porch full of excited people frantically waving to us. One voice stood out above all the rest.

"Lordy, lordy! What you waitin' on, young man? Get outa the car and get on in this house before I whup you a good one upside your head!"

And that was my introduction to Trumpet Man's wife. A woman after my own heart!

# Chapter Forty

*Violetta*

Stepping onto the large wraparound front porch, I could see that Cassie carried a wooden walking stick to steady herself. Her hair was streaked with white, her skin weathered and wrinkled, and her eyes most kind. I walked supported by my own cane in one hand and Woody's hand in the other as we reached the entrance to the large house, the door still open awaiting us. When we approached Cassie standing in front of the door, the porch suddenly became silent. All conversation ceased, all movement came to an abrupt halt. Cassie looked directly at Woody, then at me standing at his side. All at once, she let the walking stick fall to the floor as she threw her arms around the two of us, sobbing uncontrollably. We stood in her warm embrace for several minutes, aware of her family members standing all around us, silently and solemnly nodding their heads in deep understanding of the importance of this long awaited reunion with her dead husband's much loved student and friend. At the appropriate moment, Cassie gently disengaged from our embrace.

"You must be Violetta," Cassie offered with wonderment in her still moist eyes.

"Yes...I'm so happy to finally meet you, Mrs..." I stuttered, realizing too late that I had no idea of her last name.

"Ohhh, just call me Cassie, Violetta," the old woman answered with a smile.

Looking down at the little girl picking up her Nana's walking stick, staring at me with wide eyes, I said gently, "And you must be Emma Jane. I've heard so much about you!"

With that, Woody dropped to his knee and held out his arms to Emma Jane, who wasted no time in delivering a big hug.

"Hi, Wuddy," she said in a beautiful little girl voice.

That youthful welcome brought out a chorus of laughter from all.

"Shame on me, making you stand out here on the porch," Cassie said. "Come in, come in. We have so much catching up to do, don't we?"

She turned and led the way with us close behind, followed by the rest of the family. Once in the living room, we all found our way to chairs or sofas, eager for the conversations sure to follow. No sooner were we seated than we were approached politely by Cassie's daughters, Jennifer and Jessica. Jessica was Emma Jane's mother, whom Woody had met several times in years past. The only time he had ever met Jennifer was at Trumpet Man's funeral, and her eyes still held a hint of sadness from that day. While they all talked of times remembered, out of the corner of my eye I noticed Cassie quietly leaving the room. When she returned minutes later, she carried a blanketed bundle in her arms.

"Woody," Cassie announced happily, "remember me tellin' you about two people I wanted you to meet?"

"I sure do, Cassie," Woody answered with a hint of what was to come.

"Well, in my arms here is Jennifer's first born child…" she began.

"Ohhh," Woody interrupted, "that must be Chelsea Miranda!"

Cassie stopped dead in her tracks, her jaw dropping in disbelief. Once again, you could have heard a pin drop in the living room, for everyone stopped talking and just stared at Woody. Cassie gathered her wits and broke the uncomfortable silence.

"Now…how did you know *that*, Woody? I didn't tell you over the phone…*did* I?" she asked, trying to solve the apparent mystery.

Woody stood there like a statue, white as a ghost against the many shades of brown present in the room. He looked over to me standing beside him, as if begging for rescue from what had just happened. But my own mouth was also wide open, looking to him for answers he didn't seem to have.

"I…well, I just don't know, Cassie. You *must* have mentioned her name over the phone earlier today…otherwise, how *would* I know her name?"

"That's funny, but I don't *remember* ruining the surprise like that," she murmured to herself more than to him. "But then again, I suppose I *am* getting a little forgetful these days…"

Rescued thus, everyone chuckled softly, satisfied with Cassie's explanation. In the meantime, Jessica stepped out of the room and re-entered holding the hand of the cutest little boy. Before she could introduce her young son to us, Woody blurted out another mistake.

"And *you* must be Caden Michael!"

Woody knew he had done it again, with absolutely no clue as to how he knew their names, or that they even existed! But here they were, right in front of our eyes. And here I stood, stymied by the mystery of knowledge Woody seemed to possess without a hint of where that knowledge had been obtained. Yet again, the room became silent, and it took quick thinking on my part to get Woody out of this second jam.

"Woody, *now* I remember...after you hung up the phone this afternoon, you *did* tell me that Cassie had told you about Jessica and Jennifer's new children...you must have forgotten," I almost winked.

Woody's expression told two different stories. First, his almost thankful look expressed his gratitude for rescuing him from his blunders. But second, his confused look indicated his discomfort at what was taking place in his own mind.

We remained there for several more hours, accepting Cassie's kind dinner invitation.

# Chapter Forty-One

*Woody*

We lingered for only a few minutes after dinner, bidding farewell to Cassie and her family with a flurry of hugs and promises to remain in touch with each other. Violetta and I walked out to my car holding hands, looking up at the dark sky and the stars already sparkling brightly. I opened Violetta's car door for her, closing it again when she was comfortably seated.

"Oh, Woody, what a wonderful family!" Violetta gushed. "And those children are so gorgeous."

"They sure are," I answered.

"I'm so glad we decided to stay for dinner, too. That was important to Cassie."

"Yeah, it was," I agreed. "I guess I wasn't prepared for how much she's aged, though. I keep forgetting I haven't seen her in years."

I started the car and we pulled out of the driveway.

"What do you say we head over to the Toad Lagoon for a cup of coffee, Violetta?"

"And maybe even a slice of apple pie ala mode?"

"You got it!"

As I said that, I turned on the radio, which was tuned to the local 24-hour Jazz station. I caught the host's voice in mid-sentence.

"...goes back a few years! This is one of my all time favorite Jazz standards, written so many years ago by the great Cole Porter: 'It's All Right With Me.'"

Something inside me just hung on those words, and I felt a chill run up my spine. But when the song progressed beyond the introduction into the main verse, I felt suddenly paralyzed.

*'It's the wrong time, and the wrong place...'*

It was all I could do to pull the car over to the side of the road. My whole body started shaking uncontrollably. Violetta grabbed my arm.

"Woody! What's the matter?" she screamed out, the terror evident on her face.

I just sat there for a minute, unable to gather my wits. Slowly, I reached down and turned the radio off before answering her as best I could.

"I don't know, Violetta...that song...something about it just...I don't know," I mumbled, shaking my head at the absurdity of my reaction to a song I knew well.

The two of us reached out to each other at the same instant, and we held hands in the car for a full ten minutes without saying another word. I sure couldn't explain what had just happened. But there was definitely something there beyond my reach that associated the words of that song to something very unpleasant. As we sat in silence, the feeling subsided, until I felt in control of my thoughts again.

About a half-hour later, we pulled up in front of the Toad Lagoon. Given the late hour on a Sunday night, I wasn't surprised to find a parking spot right in front of the restaurant. Looking through the front windows, it was obvious we would have our choice of places to sit. I didn't say this to Violetta, but I felt like what I really needed was a stiff shot of whiskey to calm myself. Indeed, I wouldn't be surprised if she was thinking the same thing!

# Chapter Forty-Two

We walked into the restaurant. I saw Briggett cleaning a table in the back. She looked up and smiled broadly as if she had just seen a long lost friend. She abruptly threw down her dishtowel and virtually ran towards the front entrance, arms out inviting an embrace. This worried me! I thought I had already nipped this little game in the bud. Sure, Briggett and I were friends, but she had never actually hugged me before, and I was real nervous that Violetta would wonder about that. I glanced down to Violetta at my side, preparing an excuse for this unexplained behavior on Briggett's part. You can imagine my shock when Violetta opened her arms to welcome Briggett's warm embrace. Apparently, I was the odd one out. When had these two become such good friends, I wondered to myself in that instant.

"V! It's so great to see you!" Briggett exclaimed loudly.

"Great to see you, too, Brig!" Violetta answered as they hugged.

I just stood there in total surprise, not knowing what to do or say. And suddenly, in an uncomfortable moment of confusion, they stepped apart from each other, looking absolutely mortified by what had just taken place. I looked at Violetta's face first, then at Briggett's. The expression I saw on each of their faces looked strangely like the way I had just felt my own face must have looked in the car a short half-hour ago. I sure couldn't explain it, but it was as if the same thing that had happened to me in the car upon hearing that song had just happened to Briggett and Violetta in the instant of their embrace. If I were a mind reader, which I'm certainly not, I would swear that both of them were thinking the same thing at the same time, '*what just happened?*' They were both blushing mightily, looking awfully confused, as Briggett finally managed to turn and walk back to her table-clearing duties while Violetta and I continued to stand near the door. Violetta stood facing the front of the restaurant. I faced the back where I could still see Briggett's red face trying to hide behind her awkward motions of wiping the table clean. I returned my gaze to Violetta, noticing that she was shaking like a leaf. She was a million miles away.

"Violetta?" I whispered after a few moments of not knowing what to say.

She turned her eyes up to mine as she answered.

"I don't know, Woody...something...I...I can't explain what just happened," she said softly, trying to make sense out of the nonsensical. "The only other time I met Briggett was with you, and we didn't exchange more than a greeting!"

"Violetta...that's just how I felt in the car a little while ago," I offered. "Your face looks exactly the way I felt!"

Her eyes told me it was time to leave. We walked out the front door as unobtrusively as possible under the circumstances, not even turning to look to the back of the restaurant.

# Epilogue

Well, well, well! It was some time ago that I warned you all is not as it seemed. It never is. Didn't I tell you that strange things were about to happen? Suffice it to say you must have experienced some disorientation as this tale unfolded, much the same as Woody and Violetta did, not to mention Briggett! Indeed, Woody's journey was simultaneously one of confusion and revelation. You have come to realize the answers as he has. After all, Woody has been living the story in real time with no means of narrating to you what he himself couldn't yet have known.

Haven't you ever been in a situation where you *felt* that you'd already done something, already experienced an emotion, already lived a moment, already uttered a word, but couldn't quite put your finger on where, why, when, or with whom? Indeed, Woody and Violetta seem to have returned to where (and when) they belong. And they are together again. But one can only wonder if this time is precisely the same instant as the one they had departed. Can we ever return to an exact moment again? Or is any return merely an approximation of our own recollections, a flicker of our shared experiences and feelings?

And what of Trumpet Man, Thomas, Lenny Dee (aka Uncle Leo), The Performer, Emma Jane, Caden Michael, Chelsea Miranda, and the rest of the Williamsburg clan, not to mention Cassie and her family? Has Armstrong found his time's Woody? Has Briggett found Thomas, then or now? How will this shift in the nature of one reality affect their own existence within the scope and realm of what they perceive to be truth? You've discovered that each new answer raises yet another new question. And when you get right down to it...do we ever *really know* the answers to our own questioning thoughts? Is our journey one over which we have any control, or is it merely predetermined, ours but to act out? *All things happen for a reason.*

Printed in the United States
39215LVS00002B/262-312